W9-AVS-068

**The door to Aleksander's private living areas opened and he came through, buttoning up his shirt, forcing Henna to look away as if she had caught him in a state of undress.**

Heat spread to her cheeks that had nothing to do with the fireplace and she cleared her throat. By the time she looked back, Aleksander had looped a tie around his neck and still she felt as if she were seeing more than she should. It was personal. It was...too much.

"What is it?" he asked abruptly, looking around the room for something.

"Sven needs the dietary information for tomorrow's delegation." She forced the words out around the pulse beating heavily in her throat.

Aleksander threw a curse into the room and leaned over the desk to retrieve a file. Her eyes were drawn to the way his torso turned, his thin hips bracketed by a leather belt, and a low thrum started in her body. It started as something quiet, but as he turned and stepped toward her, closing the distance between them, it grew louder and louder until she could hear it above the pounding of her heart.

*Kiss me, kiss me, kiss me.*

## The Royals of Svardia

*A family born to rule...*

Welcome to the Kingdom of Svardia! Home to King Aleksander, Princess Freya and Princess Marit, Svardia sits in the heart of Scandinavia. Fresh from Aleksander's coronation, the trio are working harder than ever...and so is the royal rumor mill! From a shock reunion to a runaway princess, is Svardia set for scandal?

Discover the secrets of Svardia in...

*Snowbound with His Forbidden Princess*

*Stolen from Her Royal Wedding*

*Claimed to Save His Crown*

All available now!

# Pippa Roscoe

---

## CLAIMED TO SAVE
## HIS CROWN

**HARLEQUIN**
# PRESENTS

If you purchased this book without a cover you should be aware that this book is stolen property. It was reported as "unsold and destroyed" to the publisher, and neither the author nor the publisher has received any payment for this "stripped book."

# HARLEQUIN®
## PRESENTS™

Recycling programs for this product may not exist in your area.

ISBN-13: 978-1-335-73868-4

Claimed to Save His Crown

Copyright © 2022 by Pippa Roscoe

All rights reserved. No part of this book may be used or reproduced in any manner whatsoever without written permission except in the case of brief quotations embodied in critical articles and reviews.

This is a work of fiction. Names, characters, places and incidents are either the product of the author's imagination or are used fictitiously. Any resemblance to actual persons, living or dead, businesses, companies, events or locales is entirely coincidental.

For questions and comments about the quality of this book, please contact us at CustomerService@Harlequin.com.

Harlequin Enterprises ULC
22 Adelaide St. West, 41st Floor
Toronto, Ontario M5H 4E3, Canada
www.Harlequin.com

Printed in U.S.A.

**Pippa Roscoe** lives in Norfolk near her family and makes daily promises to herself that this is the day she'll leave the computer to take a long walk in the countryside. She can't remember a time when she wasn't dreaming about handsome heroes and innocent heroines. Totally her mother's fault, of course—she gave Pippa her first romance to read at the age of seven! She is inconceivably happy that she gets to share those daydreams with you all. Follow her on Twitter, @pipparoscoe.

### Books by Pippa Roscoe

#### Harlequin Presents

*Rumors Behind the Greek's Wedding*
*Playing the Billionaire's Game*

#### The Diamond Inheritance

*Terms of Their Costa Rican Temptation*
*From One Night to Desert Queen*
*The Greek Secret She Carries*

#### The Royals of Svardia

*Snowbound with His Forbidden Princess*
*Stolen from Her Royal Wedding*

Visit the Author Profile page
at Harlequin.com for more titles.

To my writing friends who were with me from the beginning of this series to the happy-ever-after,

Rachael Thomas, Carrie Nichols, Lucy Monroe and Rachael Stewart,

thank you for your fabulous company and your incredible support!

xx

# PROLOGUE

*SHE WAS LOST. Completely lost.*

Henna dashed at her tears and bit her lip to stop the trembling turning into a sob. All she could see were thousands and thousands of tiny little green leaves everywhere she looked. This was useless. She turned back down the narrow path and around the corner, hope creeping into her heart until she came to another dead end. She was completely lost.

She wished her stepmother had never brought her to this stupid party. She felt as if she'd been stuck in the garden maze of Svardia's royal palace for hours and was half convinced she'd still be here when night fell. What if no one came looking for her? What if no one found her? Heart pounding, she told herself she'd been stupid to believe that Viveca would wait for her. Her stepsister was only two years older than Henna and, though she didn't want to admit it out loud, Viveca was mean.

Henna's hair fell out of the band she'd tried to tie it back with and she angrily pulled at the short strands that had been cut by her stepmother's hair-dresser. Another tear threatened to spill onto her cheek. She'd loved her long hair. It reminded her of the way, every morning, her father had woven it into plaits and every night he had brushed it out for bedtime. At the top of a sob, the sharp sting of pain cut deep in her chest. She missed him so, so much. And no matter how many times Marcella told her that twelve years was too old to cry, and three years was too long to mourn, it didn't stop the ache fill-ing Henna's entire body until she was exhausted and heavy and hurt. All the time.

She turned and went back the way she had come. Or at least the way she thought she'd come. She heard a laugh and her stomach twisted, imagining Viveca's delight at her misery. The tears began to fall faster, the hurt began to throb harder and when she tripped over an overgrown root in the maze floor Henna wanted to stay on the floor and never get up.

Gravel bit painfully into the skin on her knees and palms and even as the muffled voice—deeper than her sister's—grew closer, she still couldn't move. A tear fell into the dry dirt and she heard the voice tell someone to head back to the party and soon the sound of footsteps forced her to look up.

Immediately she regretted it. Of all the people who could have found her, it had to be *him*. For a second she wished it *had* been Viveca. Not only was he the coolest boy at school, popular, top of his class in sports and smart too, he was also the Prince of

Svardia. He must have been speaking to Kristine, his girlfriend. Even though some of the kids at school whispered about what a strange couple they were, she was kind and pretty too.

Prince Aleksander crouched down and Henna scuttled backwards in the dust, as if he were a dangerous creature. He raised his hands up and leaned back. 'I just wanted to see if you were okay.' He looked at her, his deep brown eyes unwavering. 'My sister once got lost in here and it took us ages to find her.'

His words made her feel a little less foolish for getting lost, but not for trusting Viveca. The thought brought a fresh wave of heat to her cheeks and she stood up and dusted off her hands on the pale silk party dress. Marcella would kill her for ruining it.

Henna threw a glance at him, hoping it didn't look like she was staring. Older than her by three years, the Prince had thick dark hair, eyes that were warm and a smile that was easy and offered to everyone. They'd nicknamed him Prince Charming at school because he was so nice.

'Are you?' he asked.

She looked blankly at him.

'Okay?' he repeated. There was laughter in his voice, but he wasn't laughing *at* her. The thought made her even more sad because she would never be someone he would laugh *with*. She nodded, but her face must have given her away because he narrowed his eyes on her and she looked away.

'You're Viveca's half-sister?'

She nodded. He pulled a face that was so comically full of disgust Henna couldn't help but smile.

'Come on. We should get back to the party,' he said, interrupting her chain of thought. His hand reached out to hers and she stared at it for a second before tentatively placing her hand in his. 'Tell me,' he asked, the curve of his lip welcoming and warm, 'have you met my sister?'

And with that innocent question, little Henna had no idea how much her life was about to change.

# CHAPTER ONE

FREYA STARED AT HER, startling amber eyes glistening and hands twisting in her lap. She mouthed the word 'please', the desperation in her eyes tearing at Henna in a way that made her helpless to do anything but whatever it was that the Princess of Svardia needed.

'You know, it would serve you right if I refused,' she groused, rolling her eyes as Freya sprang out of her chair, arms wrapping around Henna's torso and pulling her into a series of jumps that threatened to topple the pile of carefully ordered paperwork on Henna's desk.

'Thank you, thank you, thank you. You are the best lady-in-waiting *ever!*' Freya cried.

'I'm your *only* lady-in-waiting,' Henna said, unable to hide her smile at seeing her oldest friend so easily happy.

'And you're sure it's okay? It's not too much trouble?' the Princess asked.

It would be a mountain of trouble and at least

three hours' extra work that evening, but Henna wouldn't tell.

'Of course. Now, go! You've got a handsome fiancé waiting to whisk you away for a secret escape to some exotic location in a private jet.'

Freya pressed her hands to her chest. 'I do, don't I?' she said as if she couldn't believe it herself.

'Say hello to Kjell for me,' she called as Freya disappeared through the door.

Henna sighed, staring at the literal mountain of paperwork on her desk, before making herself a coffee and settling back in front of her computer.

Kjell's romantic gesture was sweet but it was going to be a little tricky to explain to the French Ambassador, who had expected to be meeting with Her Royal Highness at the end of this week. It would be the last getaway Kjell planned for a while, because once they were engaged he would be added to the roster for royal duties and would no longer be able to be so beautifully impromptu. In fact, Henna was half-convinced that was *why* the newly titled Duke had chosen to whisk Freya away two weeks before their engagement party.

For a moment she wondered what that would be like—to be whisked away to some luxurious isolated escape, wined, dined and pleasured by a handsome man—and then laughed at herself. She had far too much to do here. Henna picked up the phone and dialled the French Embassy and while she was waiting to be put through to Ambassador Toussaint her gaze snagged on an email appearing at the top of her inbox. Frowning, she clicked on it and stared.

'Hello? Ms Olin?'

Shaking her head clear of the mental fog that had paused her brain function for a second, she spun the chair away from the distracting computer screen and focused on the task at hand.

'Ambassador Toussaint, I'm so sorry to have to ask but I'm afraid I'm going to need your help.'

It took fifteen minutes to carefully pick through the minefield of cancelling a diplomatic event with a foreign embassy without ruffling feathers, bruising egos or over-compensating with undeliverable promises and Henna did it perfectly, all the while resolutely ignoring the email that pulsed in the back of her mind.

By the time the call ended she had swept her hand across an overly warm forehead so much that her fringe had an upward-bending kink. Finally, after steeling herself, she returned to the email that had rocketed her heart rate.

Dear Miss Olin...

...trusted member of the Svardian royal staff...highly recommended...believe you would be a perfect fit... very competitive salary...

Headhunted. She was being headhunted.

She squinted her eyes at the screen to see if just

a little peek at the invading email would make it less...*tempting*. But no, what they were offering was a once-in-a-lifetime position. And as a lady-in-waiting, that was saying something. The details didn't include the name of the would-be boss, but there were enough clues in there for her to piece it together. The female CEO was internationally re-nowned, energetic, enthusiastic and determined to work exclusively on projects that had big global impacts. Henna shook her head, confused by the enticement of the email.

She would *never* leave Freya, or her younger sister Marit. But, even as she thought it, she couldn't deny that things were changing. With Marit secretly engaged to Lykos Livas, the Greek billionaire, and Freya and Kjell's very public engagement ball in just two weeks, the Princesses were growing up and moving on with their lives. They had found their partners, their *confidants*. They wouldn't need her as much. Henna looked to the pile of paperwork on her desk. There would always be enough work between the royal siblings to keep her busy...but what if she wanted more than that?

She shook her head again and whispered 'no' into the empty room. She loved Svardia. She'd lived here all her life and while she'd travelled all over the world in her duties with Freya, coming home had always been the best part. She loved watching the seasons change in the leaves of the large trees in the palace gardens. Loved the way that the salt-touched breeze swept in from the sea, the dramatic craggy coastline that looked prehistoric, and the explosion of Svardian technology that harnessed the very best of nature without destroying it in the process. It just wasn't something she wanted to walk away from.

Henna's mobile phone rang, shocking her from her thoughts, and she saw Freya's name as she accepted the call.

'Are you meeting your sister?' she heard Freya ask over the sounds of the gravel drive crunching beneath the tyres of the car taking her to the private airstrip at the back of the palace grounds.

'Stepsister,' she corrected as numbness spread quickly through her. 'No. Why?'

'I saw her pulling up in her car. I thought I'd give you a heads-up. I wonder what she's doing here.'

Only Henna didn't need to wonder.

*Aleksander.*

Aleksander was beginning to believe that his 'great idea' was, in fact, deeply flawed.

On paper, she was perfect. She would inherit her mother's Marchioness title, she was rich, beautiful, educated and sophisticated. His family had known hers since they were children. She moved in similar circles as he did. But clearly there was something he had forgotten. Just at that exact moment, she opened her crimson-coloured mouth and once again he resisted the impulse to cringe.

'So, I said to him that he couldn't possibly have

got me confused with Lady Annabelle because the woman spends her entire life looking as if she were dragged through a hedge, backwards! I mean, look at me.' The vicious comment cut through the air as successfully as the dramatic sweep of her hand down the length of her body.

Viveca Lassgård was perched on the edge of the settee in a position that could hardly have secured a single pert cheek and could not have been anything other than deeply uncomfortable. Her legs were dramatically crossed high at the thigh, revealing more of her than Aleksander had any intention of ever seeing again. The patent red leather of her shoes matched the crude colour of her lipstick, separated by a bright honeybee-yellow dress that clung to angles rather than curves on her body.

No. Aleksander, King of Svardia, was man enough to admit—to *himself*—that he had made a monumental mistake. How Henna could have grown up in the near vicinity of this woman and not committed murder would be one of his life's greatest unanswered questions.

Aleksander conceded that he had been somewhat *hasty*, enticed by the ease with which a possible fiancée might be found. Because that was what he needed it to be—easy. Four months ago, as tradition decreed, his father had abdicated on his sixty-fifth birthday and Aleksander had ascended to the throne of the Scandinavian kingdom. The day after his coronation his mother and father had left for the twelve-month sabbatical that allowed each new monarch to find their feet as ruler.

Aleksander might have laughed, if he'd been in the habit of such things. He could have ruled Svardia at any point since his twentieth birthday if needed. The fact that he'd had to wait nine years was merely incidental. He had been six years old when his uncle, the King, had died, forcing his father to take a throne he'd never wanted, but he had ruled with absolute focus and determination. Nothing had come between his father and his duty and he'd ensured that his children felt exactly the same way. Whether they wanted to or not. It was a cause of quite considerable distaste to Aleksander that he was now in a position to inflict a similar fate on an heir of his own.

That teeth-grinding thought pulled him back into the present, and the living area of his palace suite where Viveca was currently removing a cup of tea from a tray held by a server she had yet to, and he doubted ever would, acknowledge. Instead, she was eyeing up the Italian baroque furnishings and design elements that ran through the entire palace because some long-forgotten ancestor had taken a liking to the style. Aleksander hated it. Imagine having to have a conversation with world leaders about nuclear disarmament in a powder-blue room with gold filagree.

'It is beautiful,' she said lasciviously.

He grunted in response and she didn't even raise her carefully pencilled eyebrow. He had seen women like her on the arms of rich old men. Aleksander didn't judge. He *never* judged. If she wanted to throw her body away for financial security and gain that was her choice. But he wasn't ever going to be that rich old man. With years of practice, he made barely polite small talk while he reassessed his position. Viveca clearly wouldn't do—at *all*—but it didn't change the fact that he was still in need of a Queen.

Time was running out. That the devastating news that Freya was unable to carry a child to term was still a secret was nothing short of miraculous, but it wouldn't stay that way for long. The situation had to be negotiated carefully. Aleksander hated that it was the case, but he knew what the press were like. If it wasn't handled perfectly, they would tear Freya to shreds and then start on Marit, questioning her fertility next, which was unacceptable. Faith in the royal family would be at its weakest in years, so if Aleksander needed to be married to help his sisters and his country navigate such a serious crisis so early in his rule, then he would marry.

He would do whatever it took because he wanted Svardia to be one of the greatest countries in the world. His father had protected their country when it was reeling in shock from the sudden death of their King. It was Aleksander's job to make it *thrive*. And to do that, the nation needed to trust its King. And if they needed a Queen beside him to do so, then he would give them a Queen. Even if it was the last thing he wanted.

Glancing at Viveca, he was about to bring the whole farce to a close when his body started to react to some yet unseen presence. Instinctively he turned to the open doorway in time to see Henna at the threshold, tucking a look of sheer fury behind that delicate mask of hers.

*Curious.*

Henna was surprised that she heard Viveca's patently *unwelcome* greeting above the high-pitched ringing in her ears.

'Sister. You look…well.'

The pause indicated that her stepsister thought she looked anything but. Punctuated by an imperious eyebrow, it was her tone that hurt the most, as if Viveca was surprised Henna had the audacity to breathe the same air. Viveca looked *svelte*—there was no other word to describe her—and Henna suddenly felt invisible in the clothes that she had taken such pride in that morning.

'Th-thank you,' Henna replied, stuttering over the words and feeling embarrassed. Not because Viveca would notice. She was always stilted around her. But in front of Aleksander? 'I just came to…' In the infinitesimal moment it took for Henna to realise that she genuinely had no idea what she had come here to do, her sister rose to the occasion.

'Oh, wonderful. I'll have another tea. I'm sure you remember how I like it. Aleksander?' Viveca turned, as if she had every right to offer the King a drink in his own home, a wide perfect smile on her face.

For a second Henna was caught—helpless, stuck in a childhood prism of anger, hurt and dismissal that made her body immobile but her heart rage with injustice. And Aleksander got to witness the whole thing.

Viveca had treated her like a servant from the moment her mother married Henna's father six months before his death. But she hadn't had to bow to her stepsister's demands since she'd moved into the palace staff quarters. And Viveca *knew* that she did more than make tea and coffee. It was a dig, just like so many others, as if Viveca wanted to see how far she could be pushed before she broke.

That was what brought Henna back to earth. The memory that no matter what—*no matter what*—she never gave Viveca what she wanted. It might have taken Henna years, and one particularly brutal betrayal, but she'd learned and she knew how to play this game.

She steeled her spine. 'Your Majesty,' she said, turning her attention to Aleksander, 'if the staff have been remiss in providing refreshments to your guests, please allow me to take the matter to the Principal Private Secretary to the Royal Household.'

Not a single member of staff positioned discreetly around the room moved—knowing her threat was empty—but a collective breath was held while Viveca squirmed and a battle of wills commenced between Henna and Aleksander.

*Would he side with his guest and sacrifice his staff, or would he reveal Viveca's spoiled behaviour?*

'Did you resolve things with the French Ambassador?'

Anger, hot and heady, bubbled up from a well so deep she hadn't known it was there. It stained her cheeks and stole her breath, slicked her palms with sweat and *burned*. Henna told herself that it was because he had side-stepped her challenge and not because he was considering Viveca as a fiancée… not at all.

'Of course, Your Majesty.'

He narrowed his gaze on hers and, just a second too late, Henna realised that she had revealed her emotions in her tone. Unfolding from the chair, he stood to his full height. 'Miss Olin?' he asked before making his way across the room and gesturing for her to precede him through the door which he held open.

The hairs on the back of her neck lifted and a shiver stole through her as she passed the King of Svardia and left the drawing room. An apology was on her lips but he held up his finger to silence her, as if trying to sort through his thoughts. She'd never been sharp with a member of the royal family before and had never been warned over her behaviour. In fact, the only people to have ever found fault with her were her stepmother and stepsister.

Lazy. Selfish. Rude, they'd called her. And it had hurt because she genuinely hadn't thought she had been. Bewildered, she'd spent hours thinking over her actions and tone. She'd doubted herself terribly. So she had worked harder, been nicer, become more selfless but it had only seemed to make things worse. But this time she had not only been rude, but she'd been rude in front of staff and his guest.

She opened her mouth once more to try to apologise, but he raised his eyebrow as if reminding her that she wasn't to speak until she was told to. She bit her lip and wished, so much, in that moment that his arrogance didn't look so good on him. The arch of his eyebrow added even more power to an already imperious visage and a flex of muscle drew her attention to a jawline that had its own Pinterest page.

Thick and carelessly sexy, his tawny-coloured hair was the perfect blend of his sisters', and served to draw attention to eyes the colour of molasses. Only there was nothing sweet about this man, despite his rich, complex colouring, which had garnered an impressive amount of attention from the international press.

Henna was convinced Aleksander purposely cultivated the enigmatic persona that was world-renowned, but she'd discovered that she could decipher him when she needed to. Yes, his control over his temper, features and body language was legendary, but his eyes were the one thing that betrayed him.

Perhaps if she hadn't known him since his mid-teens, if she hadn't known him before he'd changed, it might have been harder. But she still remembered the charming, laughing, teasing boy who she had met fourteen years ago and who had brought her to his sister, given her a friend, and eventually a job and a home. But now the King's eyes sparked warnings like fireworks, snapping her back to the present.

'You can't marry her,' she blurted out, ignoring the threat of danger. 'You just can't.'

That he'd been thinking exactly the same thing was neither here nor there. No one dared to tell him what to do. Not usually anyway. But Henna was different. She always had been, he thought, before veering away from the thought.

'Why would you think I might be considering—?'

'I'm not stupid, Your Majesty,' she interrupted, not helping herself one bit. Red slashed across pale cheekbones as if she realised the same thing.

If he'd had less control he might have reacted to her tone, but he didn't. Despite that, Henna stepped back and bowed her head as if she had sensed his shock.

'Explain,' he commanded. Because if Henna knew then…

'Even though in the last few weeks you've taken every measure to ensure that Freya is the most loved of the Svardian Royals, it will only go so far when the press discover her diagnosis. Marit's engagement will also help somewhat, but only your marriage would provide the stability needed to ease the release of information regarding Freya's fertility.'

He raised an eyebrow, daring her to go on.

'It would be only logical for you to have your future Queen on your arm at both engagement announcements, thus taking credit for being deferential to your younger siblings before announcing your own, whilst also testing the people's opinions of your soon-to-be bride.'

He clenched his jaw. If he were that transparent...

'Your Majesty, as the only person who has been made aware of both of the Princesses' engagements, and Freya's diagnosis, it is easier for me to...' She shrugged, clearly not wanting to drive home the point that she had seen through his plans. He cocked his head to one side, opened his mouth to admonish such impertinence when—shockingly—she interrupted him again.

'And then, of course, you asked me about Viveca three weeks ago.'

She had been wasted on Freya, he thought for only a second before realising that he would never have chosen anyone else to have been by his sister's side all this time. Henna had always been there, for Freya and even Marit when she was feeling forgotten by their parents. Henna had been there when he couldn't be and he didn't like how reliant he had become on her.

'So why shouldn't I marry your sister?' He knew why *he* didn't want to marry her.

The purposely blank look that shuttered her features niggled. There was something she was not telling him and that was absolutely unacceptable to him.

'Henna,' he warned.

'You just…' It was unusual for Henna to struggle over her words like this and it slithered through his gut unpleasantly. 'You can't trust her,' she finally got out.

Her words were like a knife, cutting through his plans for her stepsister.

'Why?'

'Personal reasons.'

Aleksander got the distinct impression that the Spanish Inquisition wouldn't get more out of his sister's lady-in-waiting, and he barely resisted the urge to say so. 'Okay, but that doesn't help me resolve my situation, though, Henna,' he warned.

He watched her wisely bite back what must have been another inappropriate response. She was right about Viveca, obviously, and her grasp on that was surprisingly astute. Henna was efficient and discreet, he reasoned. He had already taken her into his confidence with his plans for Freya and Marit. In theory, this shouldn't be any different. A low hum began to sound in his mind, faintly reminiscent of a fire alarm. The instinct to keep his plans to himself was years old and hard-learned—forged from a betrayal so shocking that it still had the ability to steal a breath and a heartbeat. His trust had been broken once and he'd vowed to never let it happen again.

But if Viveca wasn't evidence enough that he needed some help in the matter…

Henna was frowning up at him, so he saw the exact moment jade daggers of awareness flashed in her hazel-coloured eyes, as if she had followed his chain of thought.

'Oh, no. No, Your Majesty.'

'No, what, Henna?'

'That is *way* beyond my job description.'

'Freya is away for two weeks.'

'You say that as if you think that my work stops when she's not here.'

'I am your King.'

'And she is my boss.'

He glared at her, but her raised eyebrow challenged him to overrule a bond she clearly believed superior to that of her King's. He could have laughed at her audacity. But he played his trump card. 'And that makes me your boss's boss, so clear your schedule, Henna. I need you to help find me a fiancée.'

Without waiting for an answer, he pushed open the door to the drawing room and several curious eyes swerved back to a hazy middle distance.

'Viveca? You may go.' And with that he turned on his heel and marched down the corridor as if he didn't know that he'd left both sisters with their mouths hanging open.

# CHAPTER TWO

HENNA HAD WOKEN with a headache at five-thirty that morning and despite the quick twenty minutes of yoga, the two painkillers, the three cups of coffee and the green smoothie the staff chef knew she liked best, it hadn't gone away. But then she hadn't really expected it to, she realised, looking out across the perfectly manicured spring green lawn as Aleksander, in a white shirt, tan trousers and dark leather shoes, waved and gave his best toothpaste smile to the international press. Objectively, he looked *good*. This was the perfectly polished, sanitised version for mothers and little children to warm their hearts.

But in her mind's eye she saw him as he had been at the Vårboll, the annual Spring Ball held at the Palace. He'd towered above her, dressed in his cream thigh-length military coat with gold piping at the shoulders and neck. He'd been draped with military decorations and more finery than half the women in the room, but he had made it look *fierce*.

Despite Aleksander's plan to force Freya back into

Kjell's arms, Freya had returned from Sweden devastated but determined to do her royal duty and at the Vårboll Henna had stood beside Aleksander, her heart breaking as Freya had said goodbye to the man she loved and thought she could never have. The raw umber of Aleksander's eyes had turned nearly black but his fury had been nothing compared to her own. She'd been angry with him for manipulating her best friend, even if he felt he had the right as her older brother and King, and furious with him for inflicting more hurt on Freya.

And for the first time since he'd come across her in the maze all those years ago, she'd had the audacity to order him to fix it. To fix Freya's broken heart and the mess he'd created. And a connection had formed between them, despite his status and her role, a shared moment of understanding. She had commanded a king. And he'd *obeyed*. And *that* was when things had changed between them. From that moment on, his gaze no longer passed over her. Each time she felt it, it caught, snagged on her and tugged. Not to get free, but to pull her to him, to draw her in as if she had no choice.

And now, as if he'd heard her very thoughts, across the lawn and in front of at least thirty of the world's press and photographers, he looked straight at her and she had no time to brace herself for the impact. The fake smile didn't matter, the way he was crouched down, shaking the hand of a little girl... No, it was the look in his eyes and even though it lasted barely a full second it was enough time for her breath to stutter, the hairs on her skin to lift and her heart to bruise. Turning away, she called herself all kinds of fool. Because it was now her job to find the King of Svardia a Queen.

Twenty minutes later Aleksander joined her as they walked away from one of her favourite charities. Founded by Aleksander, The Children's Garden Party recognised children for overcoming life-changing events to their families and loved ones. It celebrated resilience and showed the children how much support they had within their communities beyond the finite boundaries of family and it never failed to remind her of the assistance the royal family had given her. Instinctively, their steps fell into a rhythm as Henna looked over the schedule she'd been sent by the press office.

'You're running a little behind,' she observed as they made their way to the staff entrance at the back of the Palace.

His hand lifted almost to his temple before fisting and returning to his side as if he were unwilling to display any sign of frustration or weakness. Instead, he nodded. 'The Prime Minister can wait. He won't like it, but he will at least understand. The CEO from Nordact, however... Could you look into organising a palace tour for him? That would buy me, what, thirty minutes?' he asked without looking at her.

'It would buy you forty-eight minutes, Your Majesty, and if you had a secretary, they would be able to—'

'It is not my fault that Anders retired when my father relinquished the throne,' he snapped, uncharacteristically terse.

'But it is your responsibility to find a replacement,' she replied, aiming for delicacy and failing, given the look in his eyes. 'It has been four months,' she pressed. 'It is—'

'Enough.'

She pressed her lips together to prevent another ill-advised response from escaping, aware that Aleksander had no need to justify himself. So she was surprised when he said, 'I was expecting Lars to continue on with me.' She remembered the quiet, self-contained assistant who had been with Aleksander for almost as long as she had been with Freya.

'Where is he now?' she dared to ask.

'I believe he is teaching personal assistant courses at an exorbitant fee.'

She couldn't imagine it—just up and leaving like that. The relationship between a royal and their assistant—it was a bond unlike anything else. She thought back to the email she had received offering her a role away from the royal family. The job invitation she hadn't yet replied to. An email she should just delete, but for some reason hadn't yet. Shaking the thought clear from her mind, she focused on the task at hand.

'We need to talk about your...' Henna struggled for a word that wasn't offensive or rude '...requirements.' She thought she heard him grunt in response. Really, she was beginning to get more than a little frustrated. This was supposed to be something he wanted after all. 'Your Highness, we need to discuss timelines and—'

'Two weeks.'

Henna missed a step.

'Are you unwell?' he demanded.

'I have a headache.'

'I know the feeling,' he muttered, and she resisted the urge to roll her eyes.

'Two weeks is all we have, as she will need to be on my arm for Freya's engagement party,' he said, tucking his hands into his trouser pockets. He squinted off into the distance. 'She must be educated. Degree level at least,' Aleksander plucked from an invisible list.

Henna noted it down on her tablet.

'Scandal-free, preferably,' he continued, and she ignored the way it sounded horrifyingly like ticking boxes on a medical health form.

'Able to handle the press and public events,' Henna added, adding it to the list only once Aleksander had nodded in approval. 'Titled,' she continued, starting to type before he could respond.

'No.'

'What?' Henna asked, stopping to stare at him.

'No, my future Queen doesn't have to have a title.' He was peering at her as if she had started to sprout leaves.

'But what about Freya? And Marit when she thought she would have to replace Freya as second in line to the throne? The second in line has to marry someone with a title. It's the legislation.'

'I know that you might find this hard to believe, but I do know my country's constitution. Can we?' he asked, gesturing impatiently to the pathway that would bring them to the back of the palace.

'But why not you?'

He stared at her impatiently. 'Do you not consider my title enough for both of us?'

*Us*. She knew he hadn't meant it like that, but her unhelpful mind inserted herself into that impossible equation and suddenly she *did* feel unwell.

'I have a one o'clock meeting,' he said over his shoulder as he marched towards the palace.

'And I have one at twelve-thirty,' she threw back.

His gaze snapped to hers and embarrassment stained her cheeks and burned her skin.

Aleksander turned away, wondering how the woman currently blushing with such discomfort had managed to extract an apology from the French Ambassador *and* three hundred words of glowing praise currently taking up space in his email when they had all known that Freya had been in the wrong.

The stark contrast reminded him of years ago in the palace maze, where he'd first seen Henna looking devastated in a way he'd not yet experienced. It had hurt him to see her pain so clearly and instinctively he'd reached out to her.

But she'd pulled back, flinching from him, as if he already wore a crown, as if the thing created a shield between him and everyone around him. His girlfriend, who'd hated the spotlight of being associated with a prince. His father, whose lessons and teachings had been unrelenting. His mother, who'd been so picture-perfect she'd remained that way even when the press had gone home. But when Henna had placed her hand in his it had cut through the numbness surrounding him. She had given him her trust and, as it turned out, her loyalty.

'What about Sonja Hund?'

Henna's question yanked him from the memory and dropped him mid-stride towards the Palace. He thought of the blonde banking CFO who had done a lot of good charity work throughout the Scandinavian Peninsula.

'No. She's about to launch a coup against the CEO of Lungrandst and that would be…'

'Distasteful?'

'…To the world's press. My fiancée can't be seen as more—'

'Powerful?'

'*Aggressive* than me.' That aside, he hadn't minded her suggestion. 'What about Marian Fastvold?' he asked her, curious about what Henna would think.

'Gambling addiction.'

'Really?' he asked, genuinely shocked. He was

very good at reading people and he'd never seen a hint of it.

'Really,' she confirmed. 'Would you consider English-speaking?'

He winced. 'Might be harder, unless they were fluent in at least one of the Scandinavian languages.'

Henna cocked her head to one side. 'Natassia Malthe?'

Hmm… He hadn't considered the Norwegian businesswoman, though she did meet the requirements of his future fiancée. 'How old is she?'

'Twenty-eight.'

They were finally approaching the Palace building. 'And you think she would be amenable?'

Henna considered his question. 'Yes.'

'This would have to be done quietly.'

'Of course, Your Majesty.'

He clenched his jaw. 'I am serious, Henna.'

'As am I. It can be done very discreetly.'

'How? Is there some secret cabal of assistants I should know about?'

'Absolutely. And the first rule of the secret cabal is not to *talk* about the secret cabal.'

And, with that, she left him standing at the back entrance to the Palace wondering what perfume she was wearing, because it reminded him of both roses and cucumber and it was driving him a little crazy.

Eleven hours later, Aleksander could still smell it, the scent lingering as if it had transferred onto his clothes, but she'd not touched him once.

'I'll table the conversation for our meeting in Öström.'

'You can table it,' Aleksander growled into the phone, 'but it won't be a conversation. It is done. Ilian Kozlov threatened my sister—he crossed a line and there is no turning back from that.' A fury exclusively born from the need to protect his family filled him with white-hot rage. Aleksander had hated every interaction he'd had with the Russian oligarch but as a fellow member of the extremely secret organisation Aleksander belonged to there'd been no escaping him.

Aleksander had been in his early twenties when his business mentor and old friend had initiated him into the organisation just before his death. Comprised of some of the world's richest and most influential leading figures, its purpose was to support—in secret—0those that would advance the world for the better. Kozlov had inherited his membership only a few years ago but was the antithesis of everything they stood for.

'Removing a member from the organisation hasn't been done for a very, very long time, and with good reason.'

'He has been engaging in illegal business practices for too long and he has got away with it because he was part of the organisation. No more.'

'Kozlov knows too much. Outside the organisation he will be an untenable liability. So you need to be very clear about what you expect from the organisation, should you make this happen.'

'I am very clear,' Aleksander said darkly.

'Does the Greek know about us?'

'No. Lykos Livas had a pre-existing relationship with Kozlov and only approached me because he discovered my shares in the Russian's company.'

A respectful grunt came through the telephone line. 'Impressive.'

'Yes. It is.' Aleksander had hopes to initiate his brother-in-law into the highly secret organisation, but that was a conversation for another time. Now, Aleksander's sole focus was Kozlov. 'When Lykos got too close to toppling Ilian, the Russian threatened Marit because of their association. But Kozlov knows she is my sister and he knows the rules. Family is sacrosanct. I will see you in Öström,' he said before ending the call.

He left the desk in the corner of his suite and, whisky in hand, made his way towards the living area where two large butter-soft leather sofas bracketed the open fireplace. Although the cold bite of spring was giving way to warmer winds, Aleksander enjoyed the fire. The flames twisted and turned, hissing and licking over the hunks of wood, but all Aleksander could see was Henna's hazel eyes. His sister's closest friend had proven herself to be nothing other than excellent in her work and he had no doubt that she would bring the same quality to her search for a suitable fiancée.

But he couldn't deny privately that the thought left a bitter taste in his mouth. It was, in fact, the last thing he could conceive of wanting, and the pun was intentional. The only thing he needed from his Queen was a child. It would take the focus and the pressure from Freya who—unable to carry a child to term—would come under some of the world's most intense scrutiny for what would be perceived to be a failure on her part.

He fisted his hand. The world could be cruel, he knew that. Royals were expected to behave as if they never made a mistake, as if they never had a selfish moment, as if they never wanted something just for themselves. And if they dared take it, then more often than not the punishment was bordering on cruel.

*I'm sorry.*

Kristine's long ago whispered words brushed against his consciousness and he washed his anger down with whisky.

*Me too*, Aleksander mentally replied before his grief could take hold.

'I think you'd be perfect together,' Henna said as she sorted through the files on her desk. With Freya away with her fiancé, Henna's duties should have lessened. But staff kept coming to her with queries about His Royal Highness.

'And I think you've lost your mind,' came the laughing response from Natassia Malthe.

Henna had used her contacts, which weren't quite a cabal, to reach out to the Norwegian businesswoman, who had apparently returned her call only because she was curious.

'You don't think you're fit for a king?' Henna asked, genuinely intrigued. Natassia's confidence and self-composure were the envy of many a person.

'I absolutely think I'm fit for a king. Just not *that* king.'

Henna frowned. 'I know he can be—'

'Difficult? Moody? Manipulative?'

She couldn't refute the adjectives being fired down the telephone line. But she wanted to. Because he hadn't always been like that. The boy who had found her in the maze, brought her back and introduced her to Freya…was not, she could admit, the same as the man who ruled Svardia as if it were an art form.

'I can't deny that,' she said to Natassia, 'but he is also kind. He might not have the time to be nice about it, he does have a country to run. But—'

'Are you trying to tell me there's a cinnamon roll under all that bluster?'

'That is not…no,' Henna concluded, her tone revealing how unlikely just the thought of it was. Natassia laughed. 'But he will respect you and your career. And he will treat you well and allow you the freedom to pursue what it is you want to do with your life. And you will be able to use a position by his side to achieve anything you want. That is more than most.'

'But is it enough?'

That wasn't a question she could answer, but Henna had heard the curiosity in the woman's voice and knew she had her. 'You'll have to meet with him tomorrow to find out.'

'He *is* handsome.'

Henna kept her tongue firmly in her mouth while her mind flashed back to the look he'd given her earlier on the lawn.

'Okay,' Natassia sighed. 'What are the details?'

Henna rattled them off, disconnected the call and started the hour-long process of clearing Natassia and the dinner with the royal security team and the restaurant. Through it all, the email from the headhunter kept sparkling at her like a diamond in her inbox. She'd replied when she'd got back from her meeting with Aleksander, thanking them and buying herself some time with a request to consider her options. And it hadn't been a lie.

Henna knew that Freya was going to need her less as a friend, as a source of emotional support, and more as an assistant and the thought made Henna feel…lost. The thing that had made them work so well *was* their relationship. It might be unusual for secretarial and assistant roles, but that was what made being a lady-in-waiting so different. But if their relationship changed, then wouldn't her role also change? And she wasn't sure where that left her. Marit was blossoming in her relationship with the Greek billionaire Lykos Livas and had started looking into ways she could share more royal responsibilities. And now that Aleksander was looking for a fiancée everything was changing.

Fear bloomed in her blood like ink in water just from the thought of it, having been scarred irrevocably by the monumental shift in her world when she'd lost the father who had never let a single day go by without telling her how much she was loved.

Her father had been a tech entrepreneur with a vast financial empire behind him, but the day Gustav Olin lost his wife only weeks after the birth of their child he'd handed over the reins of his company and spent every minute of the day raising his daughter. Henna's love for her father was a wondrous, huge, bright, beautiful thing. And then one Christmas he'd developed a cough that wouldn't go away. Over the next year or so, doctors' visits and hospital stays had stolen weight, energy and years from them, but never love. She'd seen the worry about her future etched in his eyes and the only thing that had taken that concern away was when he'd met with the friend of an old business associate. Marcella, a Marchioness, had agreed to marry him and take care of Henna in return for the financial security he would provide.

Knowing that securing her future had brought her father peace in his last days, Henna hadn't been able to protest, even though just meeting the woman had made Henna miserable. Focused on what was in front of her, Henna had spent every minute she could with her father, playing his favourite card games and chatting happily, ensuring he was entertained by silly futures that she made up. She was able to keep up a happy façade because she had felt loss before, she knew her mother's absence, so she'd thought she would be able to handle it when the time came.

Only when her father passed it had been nothing like what she had expected. Henna had been hit with such an avalanche of grief she'd felt buried, suffocated by the weight of it. She'd been furious with her father and the world for not telling her how painful it would be—an acute betrayal, as if they had all kept this devastating secret to themselves. Because the distant throb that her mother's absence had left her with was nothing like the searing, shocking horror of losing her father. Each day she'd felt as if a hand pressed down on her chest, trying to squeeze out more tears from a well that was exhausted and dry. She'd been so blinded by her loss that she'd not seen the changes that Marcella had started to make to the only home she'd ever known. The estate had been carved up, modernised, painted and wallpapered. Everything she'd ever known swept away by a decorator and she'd been numb to it all.

She'd seen the changes with her eyes, but she hadn't been able to feel it until it was too late. And Henna just couldn't shake the feeling that it was happening all over again. She was seeing the changes with her eyes, but she refused to sit around waiting for the blow to land, as she had done as a child. No. Now, she had a choice. Allow the tide to wash her towards something new or stand and buckle, as she had before, under the tsunami that was on the horizon.

Maybe the job offer was a sign that she should be moving on—it had certainly come at a fortuitous moment where she could take pause and consider her future. And if she did want to move on, then maybe helping Aleksander find a fiancée would be the full stop on this part of her life.

The fact that it took fifteen members of the palace security team, three close protection officers, a press embargo and an hour and a half to get to the restaurant might have had something to do with why Aleksander didn't date. Outside of that, he worked very hard to make sure the press didn't find out about the affairs he did have—ones that were short-term, mutually beneficial and extremely pleasurable for everyone involved. Consenting adults who knew—and were happy with—the boundaries in place was easy, uncomplicated and all that he needed.

Anything more? No. It was off the table for him and had been ever since Kristine. A part of him hated that she was still a shadow hanging over him, but the other part welcomed the reminder. Always. Because it was a lesson he needed to remember, especially now—that he couldn't trust anyone not to betray him, even those closest to him. The past swirled, thick and heavy, pulling him into a hurt he refused to revisit, but when his limousine pulled up to the back entrance of a Michelin-starred restaurant on the edge of Svardia's capital city he turned his thoughts from the past, determined to make the most of an evening with an intelligent, beautiful woman.

He walked through the kitchen, nodding at the bowed heads of staff in chef's whites, to where the head waiter greeted him at the kitchen pass as if he'd just stepped off the red carpet. Beyond the smartly dressed man was a restaurant entirely empty of customers. While it would certainly impact on the atmosphere, it would at least allow for privacy. Privacy that would be needed if they were to reach an agreement that suited them both. Just as he was taking his seat, the doors in front of him swept open and he stood, ready to greet the woman he hoped might turn out to be his future Queen.

His gaze started at her feet. He'd only ever really seen Natassia a few pages into the same newspapers he was regularly headlining so he was surprised by the impact the sight of an impressive height of heel beneath slim ankles and shapely calves had on him. His fist instinctively curled as if he'd taken her calf into his palm and smoothed his hand upwards. The black velvet dress clung to legs that made his mouth water, the tauntingly respectable hemline at odds with the direction of his thoughts. Soon his eyes were racing upwards, over hips, waist and, refusing to linger obtusely anywhere between there and her face, he finally looked up.

And was shocked.

'I'm sorry. Natassia has—'

'Stood me up,' he concluded before Henna could finish. He mentally cursed and then, without a hope in hell of calling it back, laughed.

# CHAPTER THREE

THE BARK OF laughter caught Henna by surprise. Not for a second did she think it was aimed at her. No, he was many things but cruel was not one of them. There was something cynical, self-deprecating even, about it. Aleksander was laughing at himself, though she couldn't think for the life of her why.

Frowning, she made her way towards the table that occupied the middle of the room, sure he was muttering about being careful what you wished for. She'd known that coming here to let him know that Natassia had been called away was going to be awkward, but now that Aleksander had his temples bracketed with thumb and middle finger, she was wishing she'd simply called him.

Only she could never have left him here, alone in a mostly empty restaurant that, she thought with a repressed shudder, looked horribly bare. *Was this how a king was supposed to woo his future queen?* She stopped a foot from the table and dropped her head to a bow—the subtler form of the curtsy staff used when there were no civilians present.

'Your Majesty, I—' As she raised her head, she faltered slightly as she caught his penetrating gaze.

'If you've come to stand me up, Henna, there's little point standing on ceremony,' he interrupted.

'Aleksander,' she corrected, really not enjoying the feeling of his name on her tongue.

He nodded and she looked away, not that she could forget the way his dark wool jacket clung to his broad shoulders, or that the sheer arrogant laziness of the unbuttoned shirt collar made her want to clench her teeth together and the shock of his slow perusal of her body from foot to face had made her hot and damp and…

'I should go. Natassia sends her sincere apologies but,' she said, looking back to him, but still refusing to make further eye contact, 'an unavoidable personal matter came up at the very last minute.'

There was silence until she raised her eyes to his and, even bracing herself this time, she was hit with that bank of heat, as if she'd just emerged from an air-conditioned airport into the height of summer. And then, as if she'd reversed the trip, it was gone. With a blink of his eyes he'd turned it off and she was coward enough to admit she felt relieved.

'You might as well sit,' he said, gesturing to the chair on the opposite side of the small square table laid for two.

Henna's discomfort increased and she was self-conscious in the dress that she'd worn because…well, she couldn't come to a Michelin-starred restaurant to dump a king in her office clothes. But, unfortunately, she was tired, incredibly hungry and didn't like being ordered around by Aleksander, who—when he was in *this* mood—was incredibly unpredictable and liable to manipulate small countries. She wanted to tell him that she wasn't a dog, but instead a polite, 'No, thank you. I should be getting back,' slipped from her lips.

'Henna, sit down.' It wasn't a request and even the discreet security team stood up that little bit taller.

'Yes, sir,' she said quietly as she sat down in the chair.

'Don't, sir me,' he said under his breath as much as she had.

'Then don't behave like an—' She could have bitten off her own tongue. Had she really been about to call the King of Svardia an *arse*?

Once again, Aleksander laughed, which seemed to surprise him as much as her and completely changed the mood in the room. Apparently having decided it was safe, the head waiter came over and offered them a menu each. Even though Aleksander studied it intently, she couldn't shake the feeling that *she* was the object of his considerable attention.

Henna accepted the menu with a smile and waited while the waiter poured them each a glass of water and explained that they were welcome to order from the menu or, if they would like, the chef had prepared a special meal with wine pairings that was, in his humble opinion, excellent.

'That would be wonderful, Jakob, thank you,' Aleksander replied, gently snatching the menu from her fingers and handing it back to the waiter.

Reluctantly, she let a smile pull at the corner of her mouth. There was a cheek to his actions and a spark in his eyes she'd not seen for a very long time. This was who she remembered. Not the manipulator, not the brooding power of the throne—*him*.

'So, I'm behaving like an—'

'Only, apparently, on special occasions such as these,' she fired back, belatedly shocked by her audacity.

'Special occasions?' he asked.

'When you're left to your own devices you have a tendency to become…'

'A monster?'

'Hardly. A beast, perhaps.'

He inclined his head to the side, as if saying *touché*.

'Great, big, hairy—'

'That's quite enough of that, thank you,' he said as the waiter appeared with a bottle of wine and Henna felt a warmth in her chest, radiating outwards. Really, she should have known better, because Aleksander was like one of the very best predators, lulling his prey into a false sense of security before striking. Because that was precisely what he did the moment the waiter left.

'Tell me what happened between you and Viveca.'

\* \* \*

Aleksander half wished he could take the question back. Beneath the soft lighting in the restaurant, Henna had visibly paled. But something had happened between Henna and her sister and it was something bad. A protective instinct had risen in him watching their interaction and he neither liked it or wanted it in his life and had therefore decided that only by knowing what had happened would he be able to remove it.

'It is none of your business,' she said tightly, and he could see how much it cost her to refuse his demand.

She reached for her wine, her fingers plucking the thin stem from the table and bringing the rim of the glass to her lips. It was wrong of him to be so aware of a woman so clearly angry with him. But it was more than anger. He could tell—just as he had done the first time they had met—that she was holding back an avalanche of hurt and he didn't like it. He'd never liked it.

'Tell me and I will find a secretary,' he offered, utterly aware of how much work she had shouldered on his behalf in recent months.

This time it was Henna who laughed. It was half disbelief, half humour, and it was all honest. That was a hard thing to find when you were King and a long-forgotten part of him was delighted.

'A secretary *and* a fiancée. Just make sure you don't get them confused.'

'That really would give the press something to talk about,' he mused.

'And the palace HR department, I'm sure.'

The gentle humour lay between them, heated in the flame of the table's candle and evaporated. He could see her thoughts turn back to his question, could read the internal struggle she was having at the thought of telling him. He held his breath until a sigh signalled her defeat.

'You're aware I stayed in Svardia when Freya went to Switzerland for her degree?'

Aleksander nodded, remembering. His sister had desperately wanted to stand on her own two feet, be truly independent for the three years of her studies without protection officers or assistants and staff. And although their father had agreed, he'd lied and had secretly sent an undercover bodyguard, Kjell, to keep an eye on her. It had been devastating for his sister when she'd discovered the truth.

'I went to college here in Torfarn. It's such a beautiful campus and the lecturers were wonderful. And… I didn't want to be anywhere else,' she said, shrugging as if she should apologise for her love for Svardia. The candlelight flickered in her middle-distance gaze. 'That's where I met Nils.'

Beneath the table, Aleksander's hands fisted reflexively and it took an inordinate amount of energy to undo the unconscious action.

'He was studying biology, but his flatmate had a few lectures with me. Nils was,' she said, finally turning her gaze back to him, 'nice.' She nodded as if agreeing with her own assessment. 'He was quiet, easy, uncomplicated. And I felt safe.'

He could hear the longing in her voice, as if she still felt the need for such things—safety—and a small part of his mind filed the important fact away.

'When he proposed, I thought that it was done. That *I* was done. That my future was a home with him and a family. He was so different from the hysteria of Viveca and her mother, there was no game playing, no drama. He was quiet and...'

'Safe,' Aleksander completed.

She nodded, and reached up to sweep a hand through her fringe. 'I didn't want him to meet them. I thought they would devour him and that he might run away. Might decide that it wasn't worth it.'

Aleksander read between her words. She'd feared that he might find that *she* wasn't worth it. He didn't quite know where this story was going, but he didn't like it and he most definitely didn't like the idea that Henna would think at any point that she was unworthy. From the corner of his eye, he saw the waiter hovering at the kitchen pass with the first course and subtly held him off with a hand.

'But I took him home and, surprisingly, it went well. My stepmother behaved herself. Viveca was on her best behaviour, which simply meant ignoring us both for the most part which, of course, I was more than fine with,' she said with a smile that trembled a little. Her inhale drew the candle flame ever so slightly towards her as if it too was waiting on what happened next. 'And then, about two weeks later, I came home and the bed wasn't made. It was a silly thing—Nils must have been in a rush that morning. Only when I shook out the duvet, Viveca's earring came flying from the sheets. It was gold and long and nothing about it being there was a mistake.' Henna looked at the napkin she was twisting in her hands, her cheeks as pale as the white cotton. 'She wanted me to know that she'd slept with my fiancé.'

He had imagined Viveca callous and cold, but the intent behind her actions was vicious. During his stunned silence, the waiter appeared and placed the first course on the table, having incorrectly identified a lull in the conversation. Ignoring both the man and the food, he asked, 'What did you do?'

'Nothing,' she replied, taking a small sip of her wine before carefully placing the glass back on the table.

'What do you mean?'

'I did the opposite of what Viveca wanted,' she said, finally looking up at him with eyes that exposed her hurt. 'I ended my relationship with Nils and never spoke to either of them about what had happened.'

'You didn't confront them? At all?' he asked, shocked.

'No,' she replied.

'But she got away with it.'

Henna shook her head. 'She's a bully. She wanted

the drama. She wanted the responsibility for ending my relationship with Nils. I refused to give her that.'

He understood the logic, had now seen enough of Viveca to know that Henna was right. But that kind of hurt, that kind of devastation…to keep it all locked in and not let it out…he knew the toll it took.

'I'm sorry,' he said, for asking, for forcing her to admit such a thing, and for such an awful thing to have happened to her. He could see the hurt and betrayal simmering beneath the cloudy honey colour of her eyes and recognised that particular brand of poison.

She nodded, accepting his apology even through the clawing sense of shame and hurt unspooling in her chest. She'd never told anyone what had happened with Nils, the betrayal one so shocking that it had spread a numbness through her. A shock so close to grief that for just a moment, in that bedroom, she'd been tempted to ignore the earring.

Yes, she'd felt the hot sting of humiliation because Nils had slept with Viveca, but the deeper cut, the real source of shame was that for one moment she'd considered disregarding it. Her longing for safety and security, for a home where she was loved once more was so strong she would have lied to herself and deny that she'd ever seen the earring.

Even Freya didn't know about Nils, the entire situation over and done with before her return from university in Switzerland. And when Freya had come back she'd been so broken-hearted by the lie that had severed her burgeoning relationship with Kjell that Henna had had no time to wallow in her own heartache, moving into her role and lodgings at the Palace immediately.

How could she explain the devastating loss of a future she had believed in because she'd been so utterly convinced it was *safe*? The way that it had crumbled everything around her and beneath her and left her shaking for months after. How everything had suddenly felt less real than the fantasy of a future she had created where she would be happy.

Nils had been her future, her safe harbour and her security. Viveca had destroyed that, and she still didn't know what she'd done to make her stepsister do such a thing. Logically, Henna had told herself, it had been better to find out the nature of her fiancé before she'd married him. And she had been so utterly thankful to throw herself into royal service, which gave her a home and a purpose. But in her most secret heart she wondered if she had forged a bond with Nils because of the future she'd thought he could offer her. Maybe if she hadn't lost her father at such a young age, if Marcella and Viveca hadn't been so cruel, it wouldn't have impacted her so severely. But it had made her determined never to build her safety, her *home*, around one man ever again.

'Did Natassia really have a family emergency?'

Henna felt Aleksander's eyes watching her reaction to his question and decided to go with the truth. 'I'd say the chances are fifty-fifty at this point.'

'Interesting,' he said, spearing the delicate flesh of the salmon with more enthusiasm than he'd seemed to give his date.

'Well, it might have something to do with the rumours about you and Reina—'

'Michaels!' Aleksander said, snapping his fingers in recollection.

'And something to do with a maid's uniform?'

'Yes. Well, that would make sense.'

'Do I want to know?'

'Absolutely not,' he assured with one hundred percent arrogant conviction.

Henna failed to suppress the smile that pulled at her mouth. 'Well, I did actually try to find a replacement, but apparently it's a little harder than I'd thought.'

He narrowed his eyes and Henna couldn't account for why that made their exchange feel more intimate, other than being the sole focus of his fierce intellect and sometimes wicked humour.

'Who did you ask?'

'Agnes Ullman.'

He winced. 'Ouch. No, she's—'

'And Ingrid Harr.'

Henna thought she might have heard him groan. How he'd managed to keep all of this from the international press was inconceivable to her.

'I could be persuaded to admit that I'm a little difficult,' he offered graciously.

Henna snorted. 'I hadn't noticed.'

He was chewing and, honestly, there really shouldn't be anything remotely sexy about a man chewing a mouthful of food, but it was his eyes. He looked for just a second as if what he found most delicious in that moment wasn't the mouthful of exquisite food but her teasing him.

And then she realised it was highly unlikely that anyone had teased him in a while. Certainly not since he'd become King and probably even long before then, maybe not since his late teens, after the breakup with Kristine. Because after they had split Aleksander had become a completely different person. Henna was tempted to ask him about it. After all, he'd certainly delved into her personal history, but she was reluctant to lose this moment.

'Where did you go?' he asked of her train of thought.

'Nowhere important. So, you won't tell me about the maid's uniform, but will you explain about the significance of the honey, because—'

Aleksander cut her off with a shocking display of Svardian curse words and the look on his face was one of horror combined with a little bit of fear.

'How on earth do you know about that?' he demanded.

'Secretarial cabal,' she whispered before taking a sip of her wine.

'Bloody hell,' he said, leaning back in his chair and now looking at her with something a little like awe.

The waiter appeared and discreetly whisked away their plates, while another server replaced their white wine with a red in a fresh glass, filled up their water, changed their knives and disappeared with as much speed and efficiency as a racing car pit stop.

And throughout it all Aleksander held her gaze.

And throughout it all she wished he didn't. Because this wasn't a date. This very much wasn't *her* date, that was for sure. A tingling began at her fingertips and her heart felt full and thick as it thudded in her chest, each beat sending fissures of need around her body.

Looking away, she caught the eye of one of the security detail standing at the far end of the room, and the small smile and nod of acknowledgement reminded her that she was one of *them*. Not the person who was taken for dinner by the King. Not purposely so, anyway.

It wasn't her role to tease the King. It was—as they had agreed—her role to help him find a fiancée. And whether or not she found him attractive was neither here nor there.

'Did you…?' she started and had to clear her throat gently. 'Did you have any other women in mind?'

There was only one woman he had in mind at that moment and he would never be able to touch her.

Because what he needed was complete indifference. And what Henna Olin meant to him… He could categorically confirm that it was most definitely *other* than indifference.

The waiter returned with their main course, buying Aleksander some time. 'Aged sirloin steak with a stout jus, celeriac purée, baby vegetables poached in cumin butter and…' Aleksander stopped listening and watched as Henna bestowed a beatific smile on the waiter. There was nothing fake about the warmth that she shone on the people around her. No matter the hurts and losses she had experienced, it hadn't made her brittle, harsh or manipulative and for just a second he was jealous that she hadn't *had* to become those things. Remembering why and how he'd melded himself into the King he'd become hardened something that had melted a little under the warmth of her attention.

She flicked a gaze to him, concern firing in her eyes like a spark, which was banked before it could be seen by the waiter, who finally left them alone.

'It doesn't matter,' he said, forcing himself to answer the question Henna had asked.

'Of course it does,' Henna replied lightly, still holding on to the ease of conversation they'd had just moments ago. An ease that couldn't be allowed to continue.

'No, it really doesn't. Anyone will do,' he stressed. Henna's eyes were focused on where his hands

were firmly braced against the edge of the table. He
needed her to understand this, not because she was
going to help him find his future bride, but because
they had blurred the boundaries he had worked hard
to put between them.

He should never have asked her to stay for the
meal. If he hadn't seen her dressed like that, if he
hadn't seen the way she had looked at him…desire,
curiosity, need. *No*. He couldn't, *wouldn't,* place the
blame for this on her at all. He knew his limits. They
had been hardwired into him the moment Kristine
had told him what she'd done. The moment that he'd
realised the devastating loss of what could have been
and never would be.

'Henna, let me be clear. Whoever I marry will
have to know that love is not on the table. It is not
a possibility. I will provide them with whatever
they need or want, and they will provide me with
an heir. But beyond that? The only requirement is
that under no circumstances whatsoever will they
engage me emotionally.' Aleksander had given up,
lost, too much to allow for any other possibility. 'All
I have, everything I do, it is for Svardia. *Nothing*
else matters.'

He watched the lovely flush that had coloured her
cheeks drain away, the spark from her eyes dimming
as if the night sky was readying for the palest dawn,
her fingers released her knife and fork onto the plate
quietly and none of it touched him. It couldn't. He'd

told her the truth. He'd loved once and would never again be so foolish because he honestly didn't think he'd survive the loss and betrayal that love always led to.

She nodded, her gaze on her plate.

'Tell me you understand, Henna. I need to hear you say it.'

The look in her eyes when she raised her gaze to his was a slap to the face. Sharp fury burned him from across the table.

'It is clear that you feel the need to pursue this path for your own needs. But that is a harsh punishment to inflict on your future fiancée,' she accused, her words striking hard and fast.

'If they know what they're getting into, then it is their decision to make,' he responded harshly, lashing out because of the damage he'd caused himself. He had lowered himself in her estimation and he'd done it on purpose.

'I understand, Your Majesty. But I am afraid that I will not be any part of this.'

Aleksander pressed his teeth together to stop himself from taking it all back. Instead, he nodded once and she placed her napkin on the table beside her unfinished meal. Sliding the chair back, she stood and with a quiet, 'Your Majesty,' she turned and he watched her leave the restaurant.

It was only when the waiter arrived some time later that he realised he'd stared after her for so long that the food had gone cold. And still he told himself that he'd done the right thing. He'd done what he needed to. And he might even believe it if the scent of her perfume hadn't lingered to tease him that he was lying to himself.

# CHAPTER FOUR

HENNA STARED AT her computer screen, trying to read the words in the email in a way that would make some kind of sense. It had been two days since 'the meal' with Aleksander, which had suited her just fine. She'd hoped that a bit of distance between them would put things back to the way they had been before. But then she would remember the way his eyes had drawn up her body, heating her skin and making her heart race, how his eyes had sparked with a desire that inflamed a need she'd thought long gone, but instead revealed itself to be simply dormant. Back then, her feelings had been nothing more than a teenage crush. This? This was a different beast altogether. This lived and breathed fire, and had wings to make it soar and was absolutely impossible, she warned herself every time she felt it stir. So she'd pushed Aleksander and his terrible plan for a loveless marriage to the back of her mind. Until she'd started receiving the calls.

'*Henna, rearrange my meeting with the Russian consulate.*'

'*Henna, arrange a video conference with the British Prime Minister for Thursday afternoon.*'

She had fielded ten such directives the first day and it had doubled yesterday. So she'd started screening her calls. And then the emails had started. And the last had her screaming at the screen, causing a member of staff in the corridor to duck suddenly and run away.

From: Restad, HRH Aleksander
To: Olin, Henna
Subject: Urgent
12th April 11:45 a.m.
My current meeting is overrunning by twenty mins and the CEO of Nordstad Enterprises is already waiting. Distract him?

From: Olin, Henna
To: Restad, HRH Aleksander
Subject: Urgent—not really
12th April 11:47 a.m.
Your secretary is more than capable of doing this.

From: Restad, HRH Aleksander
To: Olin, Henna
Subject: Urgent—really
12th April 11:49 a.m.
I don't have a secretary.

From: Olin, Henna
To: Restad, HRH Aleksander
Subject: Urgent—not really
12th April 11:51 a.m.
Exactly!

From: Restad, HRH Aleksander
To: Olin, Henna
Subject: Please answer the phone
12th April 11:55 a.m.
Are you there?

From: Restad, HRH Aleksander
To: Olin, Henna
Subject:
12th April 11:59 a.m.
Henna?

Henna had left her office before she did something even more stupid than she had already done by responding to *the King of Svardia* with emails like that. She had come to the Palace gardens to try to regain a sense of calm, inhaling the crisp bite in the air and letting the sunshine warm her skin.

Pulling her shawl tighter around her shoulders, her heart turned as she admitted that she didn't recognise herself at the moment. Her behaviour was not that of the person who genuinely enjoyed helping people find solutions to problems, who drew a great deal of satisfaction from coordinating people and events in a way that created smooth and seamless transitions through the day. She'd always found it orchestral and harmonious, and it had given her great pleasure to be the conductor. But ever since the Vårboll, things had been discordant.

No. Discordant wasn't the right word. It was more like frantic, nervous, *wanting*.

Every time his name appeared in her inbox, her pulse leapt, her mind tuned into a frequency of pure static and she felt that same electric current zipping through her veins. Every time she remembered the heat in his eyes as he'd looked at her in the restaurant it wrecked her pulse and put thoughts in her mind she couldn't take back. Images. Hot, heavy, intimate images. And when he pushed at her she wanted to push back. She wanted to chip at the arrogance on his shoulders, put *him* on the back foot. Press and push until they were up against a wall and...

She groaned out loud, startling a bird in the hedgerow. She couldn't work like this. She couldn't *live* like this. Aleksander was her best friend's brother. He was the King. A king who would one day in the very near future choose a queen for whom he felt absolutely nothing.

*Love is not on the table. It is not a possibility.*

The crunch of gravel behind her broke into her thoughts painfully and she turned round, her heart racing from shock.

'Henna—'

'You scared me,' she accused.

'And you interrupted me,' Aleksander shot back angrily. 'The CEO of Nordstad has left without the meeting and I could really do without the bad press at the moment. I have three meetings this afternoon and I don't even know what they are.' His hand raised as if to bracket his temples, but it dropped again as if he wouldn't even allow that moment of self-comfort.

The heat in his words enraged the embers of her frustration and she couldn't help but match his exasperation. 'You have a meeting with the Principal Private Secretary. The co-ordinator for Freya's engagement party wants to finalise the order of events, and Sven needs the information for the delegation arriving from Japan in two days' time.'

'Why am I meeting Anita Bergqvist?' he asked, as if it was perfectly natural for her to know his every move.

'Because you need a secretary!' she screeched, reaching the last thread of the very frayed edge of the thinnest tether in the world. 'Your Ma—' She cut herself off with a sharp exhale. She *knew* that he had an inordinate amount of work at the moment. He was only four months on the throne and the world was watching for his first mistake. To know that, to feel that every second of his actions and every single one of his decisions were being watched at all times— she couldn't imagine such a thing. 'Aleksander, you *really* need a secretary,' she said gently.

\* \* \*

'I know that,' he said through gritted teeth as frustration seeped into his bones. He *did* need a secretary. 'I just don't have time to train someone up,' he concluded, evading his reluctance to place his trust in yet another person who might let him down. And Henna was here. 'Can't you just—' He stopped with the realisation that he was about to beg. And he didn't beg. *What on earth was this woman doing to him?*

'Find the time, Aleksander. And find a secretary,' she said and turned away from him.

'But you could do it much more quickly,' he called after her, only to have her spear him with a raised eyebrow he would never have accepted from anyone else under any circumstances. 'You could use your secret secretarial cabal to find me someone.'

'We prefer "personal assistant" these days.'

'Henna, you could be called God's gift for all I care. I just need—' He cut himself off before finishing the sentence.

'You can say it, you know. It's not a sign of weakness.'

'I will do no such thing,' he said, offended. He'd not asked for help in more than ten years. He'd not had to since he'd started to engineer situations that achieved his preferred outcome. But for some reason it was, in this *sole* instance, not working. What it boiled down to was that he simply couldn't trust anyone to handle his affairs in the way in which he needed them handled. And as for Henna—he already relied on her far too much for his liking.

'What are you doing here anyway?' he asked, irritated that he had to resort to such a blunt about-turn in the conversation to move away from the subject altogether.

'I was *trying* to clear my head,' she said as her short strides closed the distance to the Palace maze.

'I meant why *now*?' he said, falling into step with her, belatedly realising that his words revealed he knew that every night after she finished work she would take this walk. He'd first seen her from his office window three years before and somehow it had become part of his daily routine too. He'd told himself that it was her regular evening walk that coincided with his after-hours whisky because it simply couldn't be the other way round.

'I needed to clear my head *more* than usual.' She hitched her shawl up around her shoulders an inch but it only drew his attention to the curve of her neck and a little mole he'd never noticed just in the hollow beneath her earlobe. 'What about your three meetings?' she asked as he kept pace with her.

He threw his hand to the side, still distracted by the contraction in his body that was, irrefutably, arousal. 'I need to clear my head,' he said, disliking that he had such little control over his body around her.

The corner of her lips lifted and he'd let Anita Bergqvist wait for another hour just for the sight of that alone. The strange silence between them settled into something expectant; the crunch of their shoes on the gravel felt like a slowly turning screw, tightening everything in him. So what Henna said next came like a bucket of water in the face.

'When my father got ill…when he realised *how* ill he was, we started this. Taking a walk every day while he still could.' There was a tone to Henna's voice that was soft and warm. Yes, grief was there, but it was tempered by love. 'He'd ask me so many questions, but always the first was, "What was one thing today that made you smile?" He was fascinated by what made me happy.'

A quick trio of fists punched deep into his heart. The first was for Henna and what she had lost. The second was a reminder that his own wouldn't care at all if he were happy—only that he was doing the best for Svardia. And the third…was a phantom, a could-have-been, and just the thought of it stole the air from his lungs even now. 'That is the sign of a wonderful father,' he said the ache in his chest.

'He was,' she said, love shining ever so brightly in her eyes. 'He didn't have to give up his job and his company to raise me, but he did. And I had nine precious years knowing that I was loved utterly and completely and nothing, not even grief, would have me take that back.'

The ferocity and brightness of her love was something Aleksander couldn't understand. It was there, swirling around her in bright warm colours, and he envied her that. But at the same time he took her words as a line in the sand between them. A clear indication of what Henna wanted from her life—as if he hadn't known already. She was soft and good and kind and deserved nothing less than a future with exactly that kind of love.

'He would have been proud of you,' he told her, offering her nothing but the truth.

She huffed a small laugh. 'Really?'

'Yes. You've travelled the world—'

'With Freya,' she interjected.

'And you've bent French Ambassadors to your will.'

Her smile exploded into full bloom and it was marvellous for him to see.

'That I have,' she said with pride, arriving at the entrance to the maze. She looked to the ground and when she gazed back up at him her eyes were unreadable. 'Have you found a suitable…candidate?'

Aleksander knew she wasn't talking about the personal assistant role now and his mind flew to Tuva Paulin. They'd found themselves in the same social circle on occasion and he'd detected a reasonable amount of interest on both their parts. She was savvy, intelligent and poised. As the daughter of two prominent actors, she was media aware, well-liked and respected. She was also, in person, as cold as he needed her to be and therefore completely safe.

'Yes. We are having dinner tomorrow night.'

Henna nodded and once again he was frustrated

that he couldn't tell what she thought or how she felt about it. And then he became thoroughly irritated with himself because he shouldn't give a damn what she thought or how she felt.

He took his leave then with a swift nod, heading to the first meeting of the afternoon, which he would give only half of his considerable attention to, while the other was spent leashing his body's reaction to his sister's best friend.

Henna hadn't stopped thinking about what Aleksander had said the day before, that her father would have been proud of her. Would he have been? Had she achieved all that he'd imagined for his daughter? Whether it was the shifting nature of her feelings for Aleksander or the second email from Veronique about the job offer making her question things, she wasn't sure. But the HR director had replied to Henna's request for more time with a bit more information about the role. And it sounded too good to be true.

She would be the chief of staff to the client, mediating between the client and their direct reports as well as being in charge of three personal assistants, all of whom worked together to ensure that the client had three-hundred-and-sixty-degree support whenever needed. There was an insane amount of holiday, scope for travel, working from home options and a more than generous housing allowance provided for the upheaval. Because that was the other thing. The role was located in London.

Looking at a map, she'd realised that the client was based a ten-minute walk from where her father's offices in Knightsbridge had been. He'd worked there for two years and had met her mother there. He'd promised to take her there one day, but his diagnosis had come before they could ever make the trip. And Henna couldn't shake the feeling that there was something fortuitous about the job offer. It fitted so many missing pieces she hadn't known she'd lost in the last few years, as if the universe was sending her a message, or a gentle nudge to take her life into her own hands and step out into the world. She opened the email again and reread the answer to the question she had asked them: why had they chosen to approach her?

*Because we have heard that you are the best.*

Who would have told them such a thing? Had Freya been the one to tell them? Had she realised that Henna would be better off spreading her wings, or did she also feel that impending change on the horizon, as inescapable as a tsunami and just as terrifying?

She had just switched her computer off when the phone rang. Frowning, she answered, checking her watch. Whatever it was couldn't be a good thing at nearly seven-thirty at night.

'Henna, I'm so glad I caught you. Did His Majesty give you the information for tomorrow?'

'No, he was supposed to give that to you.'

'He said he would. It's just that we have the delegation arriving at nine a.m. tomorrow and the kitchen has no idea what to do.'

'Just call him,' Henna said, already knowing he wouldn't.

'Henna, please.' The word was a theatrical whine. 'He's been in such a foul mood for the last two days and we've already had one of the staff in tears. You're the only one who knows how to handle him.'

'That is patently untrue.'

Another dramatic whimper came down the phone line and Henna rolled her eyes. 'Okay, okay, I'll go.'

But as she made her way towards Aleksander's office she knew already that she didn't want to see him. She didn't trust herself around him. Rather than going away, each time she saw him her feelings got worse, making her say and do and want things that she really shouldn't.

Henna stopped outside Aleksander's office door, her gaze snagging on the patch of new plaster and paint covering the damage done by Lykos Livas a few weeks ago and proof that Aleksander drove people to their limits. Even now she felt her heartbeat gather in speed at the mere thought of asking him for the information Sven needed.

No. She wouldn't lie to herself. It wasn't the thought of a confrontation with the King that made her pulse rate pick up. Thrusting the wayward direction of her thoughts back, she knocked on the door.

'Come.' The sound of his frustration penetrated the closed door and she closed her eyes, gathering herself, before pushing the door open and entering his domain.

The office was bathed in the evening's shadows, the low lighting making it something altogether different than what she was used to. Logs burnt gently in the fireplace despite the easing of the cooler months into the warmth of summer. A half-drunk whisky was on the mantelpiece and she turned to the lamplit desk that mirrored her own in terms of sheer volume of paperwork. The door to Aleksander's private living area opened and he came through, buttoning up his shirt, forcing Henna to look away as if she had caught him in a state of undress.

Heat spread to her cheeks that had nothing to do with the fireplace and she cleared her throat. By the time she looked back, Aleksander had looped a tie around his neck and still she felt as if she were seeing more than she should. It was personal. It was… too much.

'What is it?' he asked abruptly, looking around the room for something.

'Sven needs the dietary information for tomorrow's delegation,' she forced out around the pulse beating heavily in her throat.

Aleksander threw a curse into the room and leaned over the desk to retrieve a file. Her eyes were drawn to the way his torso turned, his thin hips bracketed by a leather belt, and a low thrum started in her body.

It started as something quiet, but as he turned and stepped towards her, closing the distance between them, it grew louder and louder until she could hear it above the pounding of her heart.

*Kiss me, kiss me, kiss me.*

He handed her the manila folder but hadn't let it go by the time her fingers had wrapped around the top of the file. They were barely an inch apart. Surprise crossed his gaze before desire drowned it out like an inkblot exploding his iris. At the sight of it, her skin flooded with pinpricks, thousands of them, raising the hair on her arms and peppering her heart with little electric shocks, tripling her pulse and taking away the ground beneath her feet.

'I'm quitting.'

The words burst from her lips, surprising them both, and Aleksander stepped back, accidentally taking her with him from where she still held the paperwork.

He shouldn't have been able to hear her words above the roaring in his ears, but he did. They cut through his thoughts like a hot knife through butter, zeroing his focus while simultaneously going to work on the threads of his restraint.

'Okay.'

The moment he'd said it, he knew it was wrong. There was nothing okay about it at all, even though it really shouldn't have come as a surprise. But, beyond that, it was clear that Henna didn't like his response either.

It was in the blank shock in her eyes.

'Henna—'

She pulled the paperwork from his hands and stepped back, shaking her head slightly as if trying to shrug off a physical blow. The sight of it was too much so he reached for her and tugged her back to him, *into* him, and for a shocked moment they stood like that—breaths held, hearts mid-beat.

And then he made the mistake of looking down into her eyes. Lush lashes framed hazel eyes, rich with a complexity of colours, arrowing straight to his own arousal. They moved simultaneously, coming together, lips finding each other's. Aleksander didn't know what he wanted more—the taste of her, the feel of her or the scent of her; he knew only that he wanted it all.

Her kiss soothed the feral beast that had lived within him for the last two days. The paperwork dropped from her hands as she reached for the fabric of his shirt, curling her fingers and the cotton into her fists, pulling him to her, his heart pounding at the contact. His fingers splayed through the hair above her ear, cradling her head, angling her so that he could deepen the kiss, so that his tongue could thrust. Open-mouthed, she welcomed him, her fingers curling tightly in his own hair, her nails scraping deliciously over skin that was overheated and sensitive.

He laid his hand above her breast, the pounding of her heart beneath his palm powerful and impossibly fast, an aphrodisiac all of its own. It was as if their desire feasted upon each other, exponentially increasing with no end in sight. He felt as if he were being driven out of his own skin and the loss of such control was both heady and impossibly frustrating. In an attempt to leash it, he dominated the kiss, crowding her with his shoulders and body, only to feel her push back just as strongly. Deep within him an animalistic part of him roared in satisfaction at finding his equal.

The taste of her drove him wild, and he forgot everything. Where he was, who he was, who she was. The moment she hooked her calf around his leg, bringing their bodies closer, the heat of her fitting perfectly against the hard length of his need, he groaned, low and deep. Unthinking, he picked her up, spun them around and, holding her to him, he swept an arm out, clearing the desk, before placing her on it. She looked up at him, eyes wild and glazed with desire and need, making room for him between her legs as a pen pot rolled beneath the desk and sheets of paper fluttered to the floor.

One hand slipped behind her, bringing her forward against the evidence of his desire for her, the gasp that fell from her lips music to his ears. Flexing his hips, her pupils exploded, shards of jade and ochre drowned in black, and she arched her back, pressing the delicate juncture of her thighs against him even harder.

'Again,' he commanded, the exquisiteness of her pleasure igniting his own irrevocably. For a second she looked unsure, so he pulled her harder against the ridge of his arousal and her head fell back, her eyes unfocused beyond need and pleasure. The cry that came from her lips was an appetiser of the feast to come and he wanted more. Keeping her pressed to him, his fingers bunched the material of her skirt at her thighs. Hot, needy and incessant, his pulse pounded *more, more, more* through every beat around his body. His fingers slipped beneath the hemline, inching up smooth skin to the crease of her hip, as his thumb dropped dangerously close to where he so desperately wanted to put his mouth.

Henna's breath was coming in short sharp pants, full of need and want, each one a delicious scratch against his chest. He'd never felt this before. As if he couldn't get enough, as if he needed it more than air. He inhaled more and more of her into him, chasing a high that had no end in sight. His chest burned with a need beyond the point of pain and the only thing that cut through the haze of the fiercest arousal he'd ever had was the chiming of the mantel clock above the fireplace. With each toll, he was pulled back closer and closer to the present, until he realised exactly where he was, who he was—and who was waiting for him in a restaurant three miles away.

He cursed out loud. Exhaling heavily, he pressed his heated forehead to hers. 'I have to cancel Tuva.'

'What?' she asked, the hazy desire clearing from her gaze.

'The…date,' he finished, distaste like ash on his tongue.

'No! You can't.'

'What?'

The look in his eyes turned from molten lava to glacial.

Her heart pounding in her chest, Henna couldn't get her thoughts straight. 'I… This…' Her lips were swollen by the passion of their kiss. A passion that had marked her skin and dampened her thighs and…

Aleksander had a woman waiting for him in a restaurant who might be his wife one day.

She felt sick.

'It shouldn't have happened. I…have to…' She slipped off the desk.

'Henna—'

She ran from the room just as the first tear started to fall.

# CHAPTER FIVE

FOR WHAT FELT like the hundredth time that day Aleksander slammed the desk phone back into its cradle. Nothing was going as planned. Marit had returned two days ago and, while she was taking on more royal duties, she simply wasn't as up to speed as he needed her to be.

Following his meeting with Anita Bergqvist, his Principal Private Secretary, she had provided him with several CVs of supposedly suitable candidates for the role of his personal assistant, but he'd found each one wanting. One was too young, the other too old and yes, he knew he sounded like Goldilocks. He told himself that he was managing to make do with the interim assistant Anita had loaned him until he found someone he could trust.

But he knew that he was spinning too many plates. He was running between obligations, patching them up with interim solutions and barely hanging on. And the world was watching Svardia's new King, praying—he imagined—for him to make a mistake for their entertainment alone. He wasn't stupid, he knew he needed to find an assistant that he could trust, but whether he liked to admit it or not, losing Lars had cost him. Time, effort, efficiency. Aleksander didn't like making the same mistake twice and putting his trust in someone else was too damn much to ask. Because the last time someone had betrayed his trust, made a decision that he could never have imagined making himself, it had left him utterly destroyed. He had survived only by numbing himself to all emotion and he would never open himself up to that kind of pain again.

Surprisingly, the only time he hadn't felt that internal warring was when he'd finally arrived for dinner with Tuva. He'd been intent on making his apologies and excusing himself, but she had surprised him with her frank response. Tuva had been exactly as he remembered her, direct and efficient. She had laid her cards on the table and he had followed suit. She too was in need of a marriage that wouldn't challenge her emotionally and they had decided to take some time to consider their options and reconvene in the days preceding Freya's engagement ball.

She was, he thought, looking out of his window, perfect. Until he realised that he was searching the palace grounds for Henna, who he hadn't seen in the three days since…since the encounter he was refusing to think about. That he was working predominantly out of his assistant's office next door proved only that he had enough sense of self-preservation *not* to work on the same desk he would have thoroughly satiated both himself and Henna given half the chance.

Which only turned his thoughts back to that evening and infuriated him even more. He simply hadn't expected it, that was at least half of his problem. And for someone always two steps ahead it was warning enough. Yes, he'd known that he was attracted to her—Aleksander didn't make a habit of lying to himself. He liked and respected her, and beyond that she was utterly beautiful. But the kiss had gone from sensual to searing in less than a second and he felt as if something fundamental had changed deep within him. It was the single most erotic experience he'd ever encountered, enough to make him mindless in a way that went far beyond something as simple as lust. Even now he wanted to take a cold shower just thinking about it. That alone proved how dangerous she really was.

But he couldn't fault her. Henna had been right. The kiss shouldn't have happened. Not only because Tuva had been waiting for him, but because he would never be able to offer Henna what she needed. And she would never be what he needed. She threatened his emotional equilibrium too much.

As the phone rang he realised that he was running late again, serving to prove his point. Snatching it up, he listened to a stream of apologies from the assistant Anita Bergqvist had provided for him. He'd managed to arrange for two meetings with two very different world leaders at exactly the same time and had then painted himself even more into a corner by cancelling on them both at the last minute in a panic.

Aleksander slammed the phone down *again*, cursing loudly and not caring this time who heard him. He bracketed his temples with his thumb and forefinger and stared at the travel plans he'd intended to ask the assistant to make to get him to Öström, a pit opening in his gut.

The organisation's meeting in Öström was one of the most important events on his schedule. It would never be found on public record, it would never be spotted in a newspaper, it would never even be known outside the smallest of circles that he'd even been there. But it was still absolutely vital that he attended. He had given his word to his future brother-in-law that he would handle Kozlov, even though Lykos Livas did not truly know the extent of his relationship with the Russian oligarch. Aleksander had absolutely no intention of letting the Russian's threat to his sister slide and it was of the utmost importance that he was dealt with once and for all. And he refused to entrust his travel plans to someone as monumentally inept as the kid who had just cancelled not one but two world leaders.

It wasn't up for debate any more. Whether she challenged him or not, he needed Henna's help if he had any chance of getting to his sister's engagement ball with his throne and his sanity still intact.

\* \* \*

Henna folded the last of her pullovers and placed it into the bag she would keep beneath the bed until winter came back around, until she realised that she wouldn't be here for winter. She sank onto the bed, the cashmere soft in her hand, knowing that, especially now, there was no going back. She had irrevocably and completely burned the bridge that had connected her to Freya, to Marit and to…Aleksander.

She had called Freya earlier that morning, not wanting to interrupt her and Kjell's precious time away but knowing that each minute that ticked by was another spent fearing that Aleksander would tell Freya first. Not out of meanness but just because he didn't always think. She'd been avoiding it because telling Freya would make it real. But Henna knew now that she *needed* it to be real.

*'You can't!'*

It had eased a scared part of her to hear Freya's response. Henna hadn't realised just how afraid she'd been that Freya wouldn't care, that she didn't think of them as sisters, as Henna did. And she would have absolutely buckled under Freya's plea to stay, had it not been for the kiss.

Pressing her fingertips to her lips, she could have sworn they were still bruised by the force of their passion. And while she could never tell Freya what had happened with Aleksander, she had instead slowly unravelled her feelings about working in a new role and being offered this new position. Forming the words and sharing them with her friend had made her realise that this *was* the right time for her to leave. She was good as Freya's lady-in-waiting—excellent even. But she was also unchallenged and it had left her too much time to think.

She supposed, had she been another type of person, she could have done anything. Gone travelling, moved to some far-flung destination and taken up a thousand hobbies. She was lucky enough to have financial security outside her job, thanks to her father, but Henna had always seen it as a financial security that had cost her too much and had never touched the inheritance her father had left her. She really did enjoy working and she knew she would never be happy unless she was doing something that helped others.

There had been a lot of tears between her and Freya and her eyes would probably still be puffy in the morning, but some of that restless slithering she'd felt in her stomach had eased a little. Not completely, and it returned the instant she thought about Aleksander, but she felt much better. Freya had asked Henna to clear their schedules for the day she returned so that they could spend it together and it had warmed her so much to know that Freya would miss her. She was the closest thing Henna had to a real sister, to family, but it was time to find her own way in the world.

Henna thought back to Freya's first reaction.

*'Did my mean brother scare you off? That's it, isn't it?'*

And Henna's reply was the first lie she'd ever told Freya. 'No. Not at all.'

Henna's attention had snagged on the word 'mean' and inside she had protested. Yes, Aleksander was moody and demanding and difficult. But Henna had seen mean. She had experienced mean. And Aleksander was *not* it. And when they'd been out at dinner she'd even caught glimpses of the charming, easy, fun teen he'd once been, before whatever it was that had happened to take all that away.

Casting her mind back, they'd been at school. It had been the start of a new school year, around the time she was fifteen and Aleksander seventeen. The news had filtered through the school that he'd broken up with Kristine, his girlfriend of three years, because she'd moved away. Had he been so brokenhearted that it had changed him so much? If so, why not track her down later as an adult? Henna wondered how she would have felt in the same situation. She had never thought of tracking down Nils because of what he'd done. But if he hadn't…if he'd simply had to move…would she have gone with him? Frowning, she realised that she wouldn't, and she wasn't sure what that said about her feelings for him at the time. Had she been detached? Had he noticed? Was that why he'd slept with Viveca?

A knock on the door of her suite pulled her from thoughts so all-consuming that when she opened it to find Aleksander standing there she simply blinked at him, waiting for him to morph into Sven or another member of the staff who lived on this corridor.

His hair was ruffled and yet still somehow sexy and, although his hands were in his pockets, tension thrummed through the corded muscles of his forearms, visible thanks to the rolled-back shirtsleeves. His jaw pulsed as they stared at each other, and she wished for all the world that she knew what he was thinking.

Wrestling the spike of adrenaline that had lurched through her at the mere sight of him, she pressed her lips between her teeth, stepping back and gesturing for him to come in. She supposed it was silly to be self-conscious of her living space, given it was just the same as any other live-in staff member's. But feeling silly and Aleksander seemed to go hand in hand these days.

He stalked to the centre of the room, gaze on the floor until she closed the door and turned to face him.

'I need you to come work for me,' he said, his dark brown eyes revealing absolutely nothing.

The statement drenched her body in a volatile combination of heat and fury. Heat that he dared look that good, and fury that he dared ask her that.

'No.'

Internally, Aleksander reeled. People just did not say no to him—usually because he made sure of the answer before he asked the question, if not by knowledge then by orchestration. And although he allowed for the fact that the manner in which they had last parted made his question extremely difficult, if not downright inexcusable, he was still King of Svardia.

'Just for three days,' he bartered.

'No.'

He snapped his jaw shut, before he could say something he couldn't take back. Taking a breath to calm the pulse that was unusually quick for such a simple confrontation, he couldn't help but register that the perfume that was uniquely Henna was so much stronger here than he'd been prepared for.

'What will it take?' he asked.

'For you to get a secretary, I would imagine,' she said, reaching for a jumper on the bed that was part of the open-plan living arrangement and he immediately looked away. That wouldn't help either of them.

He didn't want to be here. He disliked intensely that she was the only person in the entire palace that he needed while he was in Öström, but what really pushed him to the edge was the lack of control he had over his body around her.

'You could ask for anything,' he threw at her.

'Really? What *should* I ask for?' she enquired.

'A good reference?' he bit out in frustration.

Her eyebrows skyrocketed. 'You would give me a *bad* reference?' She held his gaze until he felt the air in his lungs press against his ribs.

'No. No, I wouldn't,' he said.

A large window dominated the space, a small table right in front of it. He could so easily picture her there in the mornings, hair twirled up in a messy bun, flicking her fringe from her eyes like she did when it irritated her. A fist formed in his stomach when he realised Henna wouldn't be at that table for many more mornings.

'When do you start?'

He watched her unfold and fold the jumper in her hands. 'A month,' she replied.

'So soon?' he couldn't help but ask. He was worried for Freya, of course.

It was strange to be in her living quarters, the space enclosed and intimate in ways that were unexpected and undesirable. He looked around, realising that it was the first time he'd seen any staff member's suite. The entire surface area was perhaps half the size of his private living room and it didn't make him feel much better.

'What is it that you need?' she asked, and he wondered if it were too much to hope for that she would relent.

'I have to attend an event that needs to be completely off the radar. No press, no schedule, no travel plans, no trace whatsoever.'

'An event?' she demanded, bright red slashes marking her cheeks. 'If you think,' she said, impassioned and outraged, 'even for *one minute* that I am going to arrange for you to have some… some… *assignation*—'

'Oh, God, no!' he said, horrified that she would think him capable of asking her to do such a thing after… And then he remembered that he had left the palace with the taste of her still on his tongue and met with Tuva. He bit back the impulse to groan. He was making such a mess of this.

He gestured to the table. 'Can we sit and I'll explain?'

Reluctantly, she sat at the table and he took the chair opposite, but she still looked as if she might bolt at any minute. The only way he could get her on side was to tell her the truth. And everything in him warned him against it. Nothing good ever came of trusting someone. But he had no other choice.

'I have an important meeting with several people who must not be seen with me for various reasons, none of which are illegal,' he said when he read the question in her eyes. 'And I need you to run interference for me during what will most likely be, at least, two full days of intense discussions.'

'What kind of interference?'

'I'll need you to create a cover story and to answer and field emails and messages during that time.'

Her eyes widened. He knew he was asking a lot of her, and he knew it was ridiculously last-minute. 'We'd fly out this evening.'

'Aleksander!'

He held up his hand to ward off any more admonishment. 'I know, I know.'

'I need more information than that.'

'You don't. And I won't give you more than what I've told you.'

That he'd told her this much was more than he'd ever told anyone, even Lars, and it was costing him. The meeting in Öström was the only thing outside of the kingdom of Svardia that meant something to him. It gave him the chance to do good in a way that would not be manipulated or misinterpreted by the world's press and he valued that chance and the responsibility that came with it. He would never betray the organisation's secrets.

'It is definitely not illegal?'

'Definitely not.'

She levelled him with a gaze that could only mean trouble. 'I'll do it on one condition.'

'Anything,' he said, truly that desperate.

She bit her lip, and it curled his stomach, but not in a good way; it was a warning and he braced for impact.

'I need to know what happened. What made you so incapable of trust that you cannot find a secretary, and so resistant to love that you would cut it from your marriage?'

'You don't,' he said, his heart turning hard.

'Then find someone else to run interference, Aleksander.' She got up and, absolutely incensed, he slammed his palm down on the table, making her jump, but she did not give him the satisfaction of turning to face him.

'You do not know what you're asking, Henna. If

you did, you wouldn't—' He bit his tongue before he could say another word.

Staring at the table, he heard her say, 'I know that, whatever it is, it's eating you up inside and making you reckless. And you can't *afford* to be reckless, Aleksander. You're playing Russian roulette with your meetings and your schedule and you're manipulating people into outcomes that you think you can control, but you can't.'

It was a warning that he didn't want to hear but couldn't deny. He got up from the table and paced across the room, feeling as if he were in a cage. Henna was right, he knew that. But so was he. She really didn't know what she was asking of him. His fingertips tingled and he released the fists he'd formed, restoring circulation.

He hadn't told anyone what had happened to him at seventeen. He wasn't sure he even had the words. It was twelve years ago, and he could swear it hurt as badly as if it had been yesterday. He felt it like the fresh hell that it always was, a knife twisting in a gut full of grief and loss and guilt.

He could walk out of here now and not look back. He'd find a way to go to Öström; he wasn't a complete imbecile. But her accusation had hit home, cutting closer to the truth than she'd probably realised. He needed to face it.

'My world used to be a happy one,' he started slowly, his words stilted. 'Charmed, even. I was the Prince of a beautiful and wealthy, thriving kingdom, school was easy for me, the lessons nothing in comparison to the studies my father would have me learn in preparation to becoming King. Despite my status, I had friends—good, funny, naughty, silly—every single thing I could ask for. And Kristine. She was…'

'Lovely,' Henna filled in. Kristine had been quiet but always nice. She certainly hadn't been like Viveca and her friends, whose vicious tongue-lashings had sometimes bordered on bullying. There had been something about Kristine that remained apart from it all but anchored to Aleksander. They had always been hand in hand, despite the school rule about remaining eleven inches apart.

'You remember her?' he asked and for a moment she thought he sounded surprised.

She nodded rather than answering because of course she remembered the girl who'd put an end to Henna's childhood crush on the boy who had found her in the maze and given her a best friend. She had seen their relationship and known that it was special.

'We'd been together for three years. I think, outside of the time she spent with me, she hated every minute of being with a prince. She was naturally shy,' he said, pausing his back-and-forth march across the small breadth of her living area. 'And I didn't take that seriously enough.' The halting nature of his words made it seem as if he were talking about this for the first time in a very long time. Thinking about it in a way that, perhaps, he hadn't done before. 'I should have,' he sighed. 'I should have taken it so much more seriously.'

He sat on the edge of her bed, leaning his elbows on his thighs and staring at his hands. He had never looked less like a king to her. And suddenly she wanted to take the question back. A pit opened in her stomach, warning her that she didn't want to know, that she should never have asked.

'It didn't matter that we were careful…' Henna's hand flew to her lips. 'Kristine fell pregnant just at the end of the summer term.'

Henna's thoughts scattered, going through every single possibility in a broken heartbeat, knowing there was no possible good ending to this story.

'I told her that I wanted to marry her. I had thought about it and wanted to tell my parents, I wanted to have our baby. I…had never wanted anything more in my life,' he said, looking up at Henna so that she could read the truth in his gaze. The truth and the devastation…

Breath shaking his words, he pressed on. 'I asked her to wait for me and she said she would. She promised. I needed to figure out how to tell my parents but, before I could, I heard that her family had literally packed up overnight and moved halfway across Svardia. I…' he shook his head, as if he still couldn't understand it '…I managed to convince one of the security guards to take me to them and when I got there…it was done.'

A knife slashed through her heart for him. She didn't need to ask what had been done.

'She cried so damn much. Tears falling the whole time, she tried to explain why she couldn't have married me, why she couldn't have borne to be in the public spotlight, how young we both were, that neither of us were ready. This way, she said, no one needed to know, as if it hadn't even happened.

'Do you know how hard it is to look into the eyes of someone you love and for them to say that your child never happened? To not have a choice about it? And worse…to know that you failed to protect either of them from what happened…because of who you were?'

Henna watched as Aleksander blinked back tears.

'No one needed to know,' he repeated. 'So for a long while I didn't tell anyone. I kept it all deep, deep down.'

Her heart ached. That this terrible tragedy had happened to him and he had no support, no love or compassion to comfort him. At seventeen, to be dealing with so, so much. Grief, love, loss, guilt. She couldn't even imagine.

'Eventually my father called me into his office and told me…to stop *moping*.'

The gasp that fell from Henna's lips sounded an awful lot like horror to Aleksander, but it didn't quite penetrate the thick icy fog of the past winding itself around him until it froze his fingers and stung his chest.

'He knew,' she stated, and Aleksander could only nod as he heard his father all those years ago.

*It is my job to know everything that happens in my country. And it is my job to ensure that mistakes do not derail this country. A job that will be yours one day.'*

'He didn't…' Henna couldn't finish the question, but she didn't have to. He understood what she wanted to know.

'My father said that when he visited Kristine's family they were already decided on…a course of action.' The words hurt his heart as he said them, as he described the end of a life that would never be. For so long, anger and grief had lashed his soul, and beneath all that…responsibility. *His* responsibility.

A hand pressed against his forearm, the skin-to-skin contact a shock. Henna was kneeling before him, the sympathy in her gaze, the compassion…it was wasted on him.

'So,' he said, clearing his throat and gently shaking her off as he rose to stand. 'Now you know. And now you will come to Öström.' It wasn't a question. He had paid the price she had exacted and she would do as he demanded. 'And we will never speak of this again.'

She nodded.

'The helicopter will be ready to leave at four.'

He turned and, just before he could open the door, 'What happened to Kristine?' Henna asked gently.

He clenched his jaw and, forcing a small smile to numb lips, he turned to Henna. 'She's married to a tax accountant with whom she has three children.'

Aleksander left the room before he could see the flare of sympathy in Henna's compassionate gaze. As he'd thought before, it was wasted on him.

# CHAPTER SIX

THE HELICOPTER LIFTED into the sky, leaving Henna's stomach back on the Palace grounds. Swallowing a swell of nausea, she looked down at the paper in her lap. It was a hand-written schedule that she would destroy at the end of this event. This journey had all the makings of a spy film, which should seem ridiculous if it wasn't for the fact that every single aspect of Aleksander's life was fodder for journalists and newspaper oligarchs, waiting to make money from his mistakes more than his successes.

The stark realisation that they would have torn the young Prince of Svardia and his girlfriend to pieces over a teenage pregnancy was devastating. Her heart ached for the decision Kristine had been forced to make and it broke for Aleksander, who'd had no choice at all. She could imagine just how much he'd tried to keep bottled in—his grief, his anger, his loss, not being able to speak to anyone about it. And then to discover that his father had known. Had known and not provided him with com-

fort, or compassion, or support… To a woman whose
father had been the sun and moon in her life, con-
stant, nourishing and loving, it felt unnatural to her.
And her heart swelled with the need to give Aleksander some of those things, even if it was twelve
years too late.

Not that he would accept anything from her. Aleksander was a man whose sense of trust had been cru-
cified and he saw emotional bonds as a threat to his
control—a control that was sorely tested by the responsibility he'd felt for Kristine, for the pain they'd
shared and for the loss of what they could have had.
Henna feared that his plan for a loveless marriage
was a form of self-punishment for the mistakes of a
young man's passion.

The helicopter banked suddenly, forcing her to
thrust out an arm to the side of the cabin to steady
herself. The close protection officers were still grim-
faced and silent in their disapproval of their King's
command. They had reluctantly agreed to remain
close by, but outside the area of the tiny peninsula
of Öström.

The cover story she and Aleksander had con-
cocted was a three-day tour of a military base,
where it would be expected for details to be scarce.
The helicopter would land, before they took a two-
hour drive, in secret, to Öström—an area that had
a population of six, comprised entirely of the live-
in staff members of a hotel that was so exclusive it
didn't have a website. There had been no photographs

for Henna to look at and she was unfamiliar with the area. She knew nothing about how many people would be in attendance, or who they were, only that during the hours Aleksander spent in meetings she would be fielding any incoming correspondence and—if necessary—pretend to be him on email.

They hadn't had much time to talk about what specifically would happen when they got to Öström and, with so many people around, Henna knew that now wasn't the appropriate time to ask. Outside of managing the details of the trip, Aleksander had been neither the commanding King she had come to recognise nor the charming teenager she'd once thought she'd known. There was a seriousness to him that she'd sensed as a middle level between the two. As if, perhaps, now she knew, Aleksander didn't have to pretend any more.

Gunnar, who had until recently been the head of Freya's security detail, motioned to the headset and Henna flicked the button that would allow her to hear the conversation.

'Ms Olin, we will be landing at the base in fifteen minutes. From there Aleksander will drive you onward.'

Henna frowned.

'Don't worry, you're in safe hands,' Aleksander said absently as he looked out of the window, completely unaware of how the thought of being in his hands undid her.

Her pulse jerked, as if he'd flipped a switch in her

body. A throb, hard, fast and just a little damp, pulsed between her legs and she forced her gaze away from the cabin and out of the window, hoping that she had hidden the sudden blush on her cheeks.

'Gunnar—' she heard Aleksander sigh as if tired of having to explain himself to the head of security '—the security threat level is practically zero, you have been allowed to vet the area before anyone's arrival, so you know the layout and you will be within a five-minute reach of us at all times. There is nothing to worry about,' the King of Svardia insisted.

Only Henna was beginning to realise that being secluded with Aleksander for three days meant that there was a *lot* to worry about.

Aleksander was worried, and it had nothing to do with the fact that he was due to meet a startling array of the world's most powerful players in the morning. No, it had everything to do with the woman sitting beside him in the sleek matt black two-seater that he usually loved driving. Large sweeping slow corners of grey tarmac cut through the craggy coastline and a gunmetal-grey sea as he changed up a gear and hit the accelerator.

Whether it was because they were alone, or that her perfume was once again wreaking havoc on his senses, but from the moment they'd left Svardia his body had been on high alert—as if sensing he was under threat. And he supposed he was. Aleksander had imagined that revealing what had happened in

his past would change things between them and he'd
been right. He'd thought that it would have made him
vulnerable to her somehow, but instead it had made
the connection between them stronger—at the exact
time he needed it to be weaker.

Henna shifted behind him, crossing her legs and
accidentally revealing an expanse of thigh that he
was intimately and deliciously familiar with. His
gaze flickered down the length of her legs and his
fingers wrapped around the steering wheel instead
of her skin just as Henna pulled two sections of the
blue skirt together. Never before had he paid such
attention to the design of women's clothing, but the
wrap-over skirt Henna wore seemed nothing short of
devious. The silky lining he'd seen far too much of
slid over her skin and constantly revealed too much
leg. Or not enough.

Fighting a ferocious wave of arousal, Aleksander
forced his body back under his control, just in time to
take the last turning onto a peninsula that looked as
if it had been carved from volcanic rock. He watched
in the rear-view mirror as the security detail peeled
off in the opposite direction, heading to the smaller
camp they'd reluctantly agreed to stay in. Returning his gaze to the road, he was struck by the deso-
late and primeval landscape, ancient in a way that
felt about as base as his urges towards Henna. So no,
even the setting wasn't helping.

The dark, jagged, blackened jutting rocks, however, hid a hotel so exclusive that it couldn't be found

online in any form. There was a central building, around which eight cabins were situated in such a feat of architectural design it had become one of Aleksander's favourite places to be. He had come to Öström to meet with the others twice a year over the last eight, but this would be the first time he had come as King. It had been easier before, when the press could be distracted by either an easy-to-sell minor scandal or a dramatic world event, but as King it was different.

Not that the change in his status would mean much to the people he was meeting. More than half of them had more wealth than thirty percent of the world's smaller countries, and each and every one of them would be willing to disagree with him or they wouldn't be there. The organisation had been the secret of the world's most powerful players for the last one hundred years and would probably be so for another hundred. And tomorrow Aleksander had to convince the five highest members that he was demanding Kozlov be removed from the organisation.

He pulled into the small circular drive in front of the main building and asked Henna to wait in the car. She nodded, her gaze locked on to the incredible horizon visible from her window. It took him less than five minutes to confirm his arrival with the hotel, the arrival of the other guests and to request that dinner be sent to the cabin in an hour's time.

He returned to the car and drove it around to the cabin at the furthest edge of the rocky outcrop. He was out of the car and halfway to her door when she thrust it open to stand and stare at the end of the peninsula, where grey and white waves crashed against black rock. Her mouth was open, shock, surprise and delight all clear in her gaze.

The wind had blown her fringe back, away from her forehead and wisps of hair whipped around her. She reminded him of a Vettriano painting, as if she stood strong and alone in the eye of a storm, preyed upon by his voyeurism. Then she looked at him and everything he'd been trying to deny rushed to the surface—want, desire, hit him hard and he knew that he'd made a monumental mistake in bringing her here.

Standing by the floor-to-ceiling window at the edge of the seemingly simple cabin that she was set to share with Aleksander for the next three nights, Henna shivered, and it had nothing to do with the gentle heat inside and everything to do with the way that the last third of the cabin hung away from the rocky outcrop of the peninsula and directly above the swelling sea beneath. The waves were relentless, hurling themselves dramatically against the rocky harbour curving around to her left.

She'd noticed that there were other cabins, but the distance between them all was surprisingly vast. The sense of isolation here was like nothing she'd ever experienced and that she was sharing it with a man who had driven her almost to an orgasm when his thumb barely touched her thigh sent blood and sparks rushing around her body in equal measure.

The single-storey cabin was surprisingly compact. All on one floor, the larger part of the cabin on the land end housed the two bedrooms, each with windows that displayed more of the dark and twisted coastline, along with the most exquisite bathroom Henna had ever seen. At the end of a room covered in bronzed golden tiles was the largest bath she'd ever seen, pressed right up against the window—the only thing separating the bather from the sea.

She'd been staring at it when Aleksander had called her to the table where their evening meal had been served. Dinner had been silent, the delectable food lost on Henna as her stomach roiled as much as the waves. Cured fish, celeriac remoulade, gently pickled beets, caviar—it was as if the chef had known her favourite things and brought them together in a dish that should have torn her attention from the man opposite her, but didn't. The silence was building between them into something that had become impossibly loud and she really didn't know what would break it.

She saw his reflection in the glass behind her, saw the whisky he offered her.

'Drink with me?'

His request was strange to hear when, before, he would simply have demanded. She reached for the glass, avoiding his fingers as she retrieved it from his grasp. The cut crystal was still warm from the palm of his hand, her skin, her body, instinctively seeking it out.

She refused to meet his gaze, instead turning back to look out at the sea as she took a sip of the whisky and all she could think of was that she would never see this incredible coastline again. She would never come to this unimaginable hotel again. She would never be alone with a man as powerful and devastating as Aleksander again. It had become an urgent refrain in her mind and she couldn't make it stop. It hurt, and it was loud, and she was tired of fighting the desperate need she had to feel his hands on her skin, to let him finish what he'd started in his office on his desk.

Maybe then it would stop, she lied to herself. Maybe then she wouldn't react to just the thought of him, she wouldn't pant his name in the midnight hours from dreams that had fuelled night sweats. Maybe then she would finally be able to say goodbye and take up the promise of the next phase of her life in a new job and a new city.

She bent her head over her glass of whisky, defeated by her desires, and just when she was about to give up, to run away and hide in her room, she felt the faintest trace of his breath against the back of her neck. Heat exploded between her legs and her heart raced as if she were running, long and hard towards a finish line that felt impossible to even consider. First it was his breath, then it was the pad of his thumb, pressing lightly at the bottom of her hairline, down her spine to the collar of her silk shirt. She felt the skin flush at her cheeks and between her breasts, and thought she heard him curse, but the pounding of her pulse was so loud in her head she wasn't sure.

Her nipples pebbled beneath the oyster silk of her shirt, cold and aching for his touch, while the heat of his body drenched her from behind, a tantalising promise of what could be. She turned beneath his touch, his palm cupping her neck, and they were finally face to face with barely an inch between them.

The moment their eyes locked, she wished she could look away. The heat in his gaze burned so hot she felt it soul deep and knew she would never be the same again. She began to tremble and even the gentle warmth of his palm on her neck couldn't steady her.

He cursed and drew her towards the wood burner in the centre of the living area. He took plush pillows and soft throws from the sofa and chairs and gently led her to the floor. She wanted to tell him that she wasn't cold. Wanted to tell him that only one thing would make the trembling stop, but she couldn't form the words and once again Aleksander pressed a glass of whisky into her hands and she drank from it as she couldn't from him.

Aleksander shifted back on the floor so that he rested against the sofa opposite to where he had led Henna closest to the heat of the fire—even though he was half convinced that she hadn't been trembling from the cold.

Elbows on bent knees, he watched her drink from the glass of whisky, her eyes shielded from his gaze by the turn of her face towards the fire. Slowly the shakes racking her body began to lessen and with it a little of the concern in his chest, but not enough.

'Are you okay?' he asked.

She nodded, but he needed more. 'I need to hear it, Henna.'

She looked away from the fire and pierced him with her gaze. 'I'm okay.'

Her words were steady, but her breathing was too controlled to be natural. He ran his hand across his forehead and threaded his fingers into his hair and gripped. He needed to hold something because Henna would see that she wasn't the only one trembling. He'd felt it in his fingers as she'd turned in his hand; her skin against his had been almost too much for him to bear. And while she was brave enough to wear her desire, to own it, he knew instinctively that should he betray just how much need he felt for her they would both burn that night.

She cleared her throat. 'You've been here before?'

'Yes,' he said, ignoring the train of his thoughts.

'So, this is a regular thing, these meetings?' she asked, reaching for her glass, her fingers shaking less.

In that moment he doubted he would ever come back here again. His request to move the meetings elsewhere would be granted without question. But he'd never be able to look out of that window again without seeing Henna's head bowed, without feeling her skin beneath his touch, hearing the hitch in her breathing hardening his arousal to the point of near pain.

'Twice a year in person,' he replied, forcing the words out through the haze of desire he was taunting himself with.

'Huh,' she said, swallowing a delicate mouthful of the rich amber alcohol he'd poured for her, his tongue curling in his mouth as he imagined that she'd taste of the orange peel, smoke and sea salt the whisky was renowned for.

'What?' he asked, trying to distract himself from needing to taste her.

'You have a secret cabal of billionaires.'

His gaze left her lips, jerked up to her eyes, twinkling bright with tease, and he barked out a laugh. His reaction made her smile and for a moment they shared a lightness that banked the tension from before.

'I will neither confirm nor deny,' he said, the smile on his lips forming the tone of his words.

'Because the first rule of the cabal is—'

'Not to talk about the cabal.'

He reached for his own glass, not because he wanted to drink but because he needed to taste her, and this was as close as he could let himself get. He could lie and tell himself that the reason he couldn't touch her was because of her friendship with Freya, or because they worked together...

but he hadn't lied to himself for a very long time. The truth was that Henna already challenged his emotions. He had made decisions based on what she would think or do, he had created a charity for children that had been inspired by the loss she had overcome as a young girl because she had been there, entwined with his emotions, for years. He threw the whisky back, relishing the burn of alcohol as a punishment. Because, no matter how much he knew she was a risk to him, he still wanted her. And when he looked back to Henna, he saw the same need in her eyes.

She had to know. She had to understand.

'I can't give you what you want, Henna.'

'Who are you to tell me what I want?'

'Your King,' he growled.

'You're the boy who found me in the maze. To me, you will always be that first.' Rather than tearing a strip off him for his arrogance, her tone was simple, sincere and it cut him off at the knees.

'You're trying to avoid the issue,' he warned, even though it was he who was hiding.

'I don't think I am,' she said, sitting up straighter against the sofa. 'We started something in your office and…' despite the blush of discomfort painting her cheeks a rosy pink, she pressed on '…and I want you to finish it.'

Aleksander cursed. He almost shook from the need to cross the distance between them, lay her on her back and feast on her as she wished, indulge her every delight and lavish her in pleasure. He fisted his hand to stop himself from reaching for her. She deserved more than that.

'You would be happy with that? One night?' He watched as her pupils bled out into the thinnest of amber rings. 'You would let me into your body,' he asked, his stomach tightening around the words, the images it conjured, the *feelings*, 'knowing that I would then go on to marry another?'

At that her skin blanched. He had been right. She might want him, she might even have the same wild need that cried and lashed in her chest as it did in his, but she wasn't ready for what she wanted. She wasn't prepared for the consequences of what she wanted. Yet neither could he leave her like that— poised on the same precipice, hurting and wanting and needing.

'But,' he said, damning himself to hell, 'if you want, I can finish what I started.'

Her head jerked up, her eyes burning with the reflection of flames from the wood burner, heat from the whisky and need from the deepest part of her— he recognised that it matched his own. And in that second he realised that he needed this as much as she did. He needed it more than his next breath.

He put down the glass in his hand, knowing it wasn't the alcohol that would satiate his thirst. 'Let me taste you,' he asked, watching the colour flood her cheeks. 'Let me drink from you,' he all but begged. 'Let me bring you pleasure.'

\* \* \*

His words turned a key to a locked box she'd not known was in her mind. It unleashed images that cascaded like an erotic kaleidoscope across her mind's eye, all the while unable to tear her gaze away from the promise in Aleksander's eyes.

'Yes.' The word poured from her lips like the whisky they were drinking, heady, intoxicating, powerful. But she wasn't mindless with it. She knew what he was offering—and, more importantly, what he wasn't. She knew that things would change between them, but hadn't they already? She was leaving her job with his family. She would be leaving the country too. They were already past the point of no return, but what that meant beyond what he was offering her tonight she would consider later. For now, she wanted to indulge in everything he had asked.

Aleksander heaved in a breath as if he were surprised that she'd agreed to his request. With one leg stretched out before him and the other bent, supporting the arm crooked on his knee, he looked more like a rake than a king. His eyes had become ferocious with intent and he looked as if he were battling an internal war.

'Are you sure?' he asked, his eyes blazing.

'Absolutely,' she replied with soul deep conviction.

Her heart pounded in her chest as he unfurled from where he leaned against the chair opposite and prowled to where she sat, hands fisting in the thick sheepskin rug, holding herself back and utterly destroyed by the intent in his gaze.

He leaned over her, dominating her not with aggression but the force of his passion.

'You can never wear this skirt in front of me again.'

'Wh-wh-what?' she asked, the word stuttering through the shakes that had returned to her body.

His hand swept up her thigh and slipped between the gap in the wrap-over skirt, his skin against hers a delicious friction, her body instinctively unwinding and pressing closer to his, bringing her chest closer to his. Aleksander's eyes had never left her face, as if he were fascinated with her every expression, every reaction to his touch. Her head drifted backwards as her lips opened on a gasp beneath his, he inhaled as if trying to capture her exhale.

One hand had bunched the skirt at her thigh, while his other slipped to the damp heat between her legs. He closed his eyes and cursed, before conquering her mouth with his, the shocking thrust of his tongue the most that he would give her, filling her in the way he had refused to, but still sending her higher than Henna had ever been before.

All too soon the kiss ended, as Aleksander tore his mouth from hers. For a moment she felt such an acute loss she couldn't breathe, until he leaned back, gently spreading her legs, her skirt falling either side of her thighs. Instinctively she tried to press them closed.

'There is no need to hide from me,' he said gently. 'Unless you would like me to stop?'

'No. No, don't stop…don't…' She didn't need to finish her sentence. All of his considerable focus was on removing her panties, all the while staring at her as if he had never seen anything more beautiful. He made her feel that.

He bent down, his palm snaking around her ankle, sweeping up over her calf, sending goosebumps across her skin—her legs, her stomach, her breasts—and she felt them like little electric shocks across her heart, making her breathless as she forced oxygen around the starbursts.

Her eyes drifted closed as he placed kisses on the inside of her thighs, painting fireworks on the backs of her eyes. The first delicious sweep of his tongue curved her body, her hips raising beneath his palms and his mouth, her back arching as she felt the gentle growl of his own delight through his tongue to her body.

*Oh, God.*

He kissed, teased and sucked her clitoris, sending shivers through her body, hurtling her towards a climax she half feared. His thumb gently hooked on her entrance, pulling ever so slightly before he filled her with his fingers. Her breath became urgent, her legs shifting restlessly, her hands fisting his hair, holding her to him when he growled his delight, pushing him from her when he stopped. She wasn't sure any more.

*Let me taste you.*

*Let me drink you.*

*Let me bring you…*

Her orgasm took her by surprise, exploding through her body like a meteorite, decimating any thought or sense she had. When she opened her eyes she was looking at the velvety sky above Öström, the stars myriad and beautiful, and she felt herself bright and burning as strong as any one of them. She felt both boundless but tethered, safe and protected. It was only then that she realised Aleksander was still holding her to him.

# CHAPTER SEVEN

WATER SLUICED OVER Aleksander's heated skin. Eight hours after he'd brought Henna to orgasm and then put her to bed, *alone*, his body was still burning for her, his breath was still catching in his lungs and he could absolutely *not* go into his meeting like this.

*Damn it.*

He'd kept the curse in, but it was a loud shout in his mind. Soaping up his hands, he swept them across his body efficiently, until he came to the jut of his erection and groaned. The slippery lubricant of the soap was too much. He had denied himself pleasure yesterday in favour of hers, and he would make the same decision over and over again. But as he firmed his grip on his arousal his hips surged against his will, one hand braced against the golden tiles of the bathroom, the other gliding to the tip of his penis, circling the head and sliding back down, and this time the groan fell in with the rush of water pounding down against his skin.

Henna's eyes flashed in his mind, the way her

thighs had parted for him, the damp heat between her legs, the taste of her, woman and sensuality, dripping on his tongue… He cursed again and he pressed his forehead against the tiles, the cool ceramic leaching the heat from his fevered brow, his breath coming in pants, harsh in comparison to the melodic litany of Henna's from the night before. The way her cheeks had flushed as her climax grew nearer and nearer had Aleksander fisting the base of his shaft, a small pearlescent bead joining the drops of water against the bruised head of his need. But it was the memory of how she had fallen apart on his tongue, how she had let him hold her as her orgasm racked her body, that finally drew his own from him, his muscles corded, thighs locked and gut tight as he came.

By the time he opened his eyes the water had washed away the evidence of his need, making him a little more clear-headed, thankfully. Until he'd dressed and made his way towards the kitchen and he saw Henna at the table, head bent over the laptop she had brought with her. She had swept her hair into a messy bun and in doing so exposed the length of her neck, and instantly he was transported back to last night, to the feel of her skin beneath his fingers as he traced—

'Coffee?'

'Yes,' he replied without missing a beat, even as his heart tripped over itself to catch up. She stood from the table, approached a coffee machine that hissed and spat, and magicked an espresso without looking him in the eye. Clenching his jaw, he fought the instinct to reach for her chin and turn her face to his so that he could see what he needed to. That she was all he could think about when he should be planning Kozlov's downfall was dangerous and that she affected him so after what little they had shared was unacceptable. She threatened his focus and that was dangerous. To be the man he needed to be, the King his people needed, it was absolutely vital that he remained unaffected at *every* level. He had given her what he could last night and there would be no more, and with that thought he left the cabin.

Klaus Brandt stood by the open window, blowing the smoke from his cigar out into the world, much to the disapproval of Olena Kelinski. The tension between the two was simmering, as it usually did whenever they were in the same room, but considerably less than when Ilian Kozlov was present. The Russian oligarch had the uncanny ability to ratchet up the tension with even the most mild-mannered of people, Sakura Maki being the perfect example. Aleksander rubbed at the dull tension at his temples, trying to focus on the most important matter for their consideration.

'It won't be easy,' Sakura warned.

'When did we ever shy away from hard work?' he growled, drawing an assessing look from Javier Casas, the Spaniard with an incalculable net worth.

'Something you want to share with the group?' Javier teased.

'Not particularly,' Aleksander groused.

'She's very pretty,' Olena's rich Ukrainian accented voice purred.

Aleksander's head whipped up. 'She is none of your concern.'

Olena inclined her head, accepting his possessiveness over Henna.

The lower-level members of the organisation came from the UN, the IMF, Presidents, Prime Ministers, royalty and billionaires. But the group in this room comprised of the highest members. Every person had more money than a third of the world's lowest income population, *each*. But all of them were united in one purpose: to use this organisation to redistribute the better part of that wealth where needed, to support initiatives that were denied backing because they didn't know the right people, or weren't prepared to offer the right investment incentive. Each and every person in the higher echelons of the organisation had a driving desire to see the world improve, economically, ecologically, technologically. Apart from Kozlov.

'Revoking a membership hasn't been done in over eighty years,' Klaus said on a plume of blue smoke.

'The man is a menace,' Javier observed, distaste clear in his tone.

'I'll allow that he's not a person I would have chosen, but the rules are the rules. Membership is passed down before the death of a previous member and their choice is inviolable,' the German replied.

It was a way to keep the numbers steady and the organisation circumspect. There were certain criteria that must be met before the membership could be ratified, but Kozlov's predecessor had been an ornery bastard and Aleksander couldn't help but think he had chosen the Russian on purpose.

'He skates too close to the edge,' Sakura insisted.

Olena huffed. 'Now is not the time for niceties. His dealings are illegal, his manner offensive and I'm appalled that it's taken us this long to consider ousting him.'

'In the past, members have done much worse,' Javier reminded them.

'And for an organisation determined to positively affect the future of the world, we might be putting too much stock *in the past*. Kozlov threatened,' Aleksander said, his tone forbidding, 'my *sister*.'

Slowly, one by one, each member nodded their consent to his removal.

'But how?' asked Klaus.

'There are ways,' Olena said, not so cryptically.

'The Greek, Livas,' Javier asked. 'He gave you his shares in Kozlov's company?'

'Yes, and combined with mine, we could have used them to bribe him to leave,' confirmed Aleksander. 'But the moment Ilian realised he'd lost the controlling shares of his company, he sold out.'

'What's he playing at?' Klaus demanded. 'He's

been parading that company around like it was his firstborn.'

'Well, it's orphaned now.'

The group digested that as they realised they'd lost their only decent bargaining chip.

'We could—'

'No,' the others said unanimously when Klaus began to offer what they all knew would be highly illegal and downright violent.

Aleksander glanced at his watch. 'Let's take a break and meet back here in an hour.'

Henna had left the cabin when the staff had arrived to set up lunch. She told herself that the necessary secrecy surrounding this visit meant she hadn't wanted to be seen, but that wasn't the reason she had come out to the furthest edge of the peninsula and the view that had bewitched her on first sight. Salt burned her tongue as she breathed in each wave that crashed against the rocks at her feet.

Last night had felt like that. Waves, crashing over her, drenching her in a pleasure she'd never experienced before. It had never been like that with Nils. No, Aleksander was raw and powerful like the force of nature she was witnessing now. He had drawn a line between what would and wouldn't happen between them, but he had not held back. It had been a passionate onslaught that still sent tremors of pleasure through her body even now.

But, no matter how much he had given her last

night, it wasn't enough. Everything in her roared
with need and she wanted to fight him, make him
change his mind, make him see that there was so
much more than he was limiting himself to. Not with
her, no. Henna wasn't naïve enough to think that
they could ever be more than these stolen moments.
He was a king and she—simply the girl he'd picked
up from the floor of the maze in his garden one day
many years ago.

The crunch of footsteps behind her startled her
and she spun round to face Aleksander, who seemed
surprised by the emotion she knew was in her eyes.
He stepped towards her. For a moment they stared
at each other, joined in the knowledge that they both
saw what the other was trying to hide. The want, the
longing. Henna realised that for her it had always
been there, and in that moment she believed that it
always would be.

She opened her mouth, wanting to say something,
wanting him to know, but he interrupted her, as if
he'd known and was refusing to hear it.

'Lunch is ready.'

Ten minutes later she was sitting at a table filled
with coal-roasted fish, sea vegetable salad, perfectly
toasted rye bread sliced so thinly and a brooding
king. His arms were crossed, head turned out towards the sea and body so tense the only two things
that moved were the finger tapping out a catastrophic
rhythm at his elbow and the muscle flexing in his

jaw. He'd been like that ever since he'd piled his plate with food he hadn't yet touched.

She sighed and put down her knife and fork. 'Can I help?' she asked, hunger completely forgotten.

'Help?' he queried, pinning her with that mahogany gaze.

'I have very little experience with the kind of world domination you're planning,' she only half joked, 'but perhaps I could…offer a different perspective?'

He seemed to consider her question seriously, which surprised her.

'I…believe that we're at a stalemate,' he hedged.

'Okay.' She nodded, wondering if he'd continue.

'We have…a problem that we need to solve.'

'Aleks,' she said softly, 'you could continue to be cryptic and all cabalesque, or you could simply trust me enough to tell me what's going on so that I might genuinely be able to help.'

His eyes flared as if fighting a years-old instinct to secrecy, but when he pushed his plate out of the way she knew he'd given up the fight. He explained about the organisation, how he'd been approached by a business mentor he'd encountered at university in London. How they had become fast friends and, until his death, Aleksander hadn't known a single thing about the secret organisation. The fondness with which he spoke of his mentor made Henna glad that Aleksander had met someone who had perhaps helped him to heal a bit. His mentor had been in the upper echelon of this organisation, and in taking his place Aleksander was given access to some of the world's greatest financial, political and scientific minds. For the most part, members had the same goal—to do everything they could to ensure the future stability of the world as a whole, rather than focusing on any country. But then came Kozlov. A man whose business dealings were barely legal, whose personal dealings were vicious, and when they weren't they were lecherous. The only satisfaction Aleksander had *ever* had when dealing with him had been obtaining controlling shares in his precious company.

'He is not a reflection of our values and each and every month he seems to get worse. He threatened Marit when Lykos came too close to taking over his company,' Aleksander concluded.

Henna's fury that Marit could have been in danger from this man was fierce, he could see it blazing in her eyes. Her desire to protect his family floored him. He forced his mind back to the conversation. 'We thought the easiest way to bring him to heel would be via his company.'

'How did you end up with the controlling part of his shares?'

'I won a large section of them from Kozlov playing at cards.'

'You play cards?'

'I am very good at hiding my vices,' he said, the double entendre out of his mouth before he could stop it, the words landing between them both true and poignant.

Henna blinked, whatever she had been about to say stalled by his careless response.

'And Lykos gave me his. Together they would have been enough to force Kozlov's hand.'

'But because he sold it, the company is no longer a way to punish him.'

'Yes.'

She frowned and sat back in her chair. 'You can't punish bullies,' she stated.

He frowned. 'What do you mean?'

'Kozlov is a bully, like Viveca. He is looking for a fight, always. And you will never win while you give him what he expects.'

Aleksander considered her words, unable to forget what she'd told him about her stepsister. 'Go on,' he encouraged.

'So…' She sighed, looking over his shoulder in concentration. There was a little furrow between her brows that he wanted to smooth with his thumb. He could have watched her think all day. And when he caught himself thinking that he mentally slapped himself. 'You want him to go, but you can't terminate his membership because of the rules.' He nodded. 'So…you make leaving his idea.'

'That's what we were trying to do with his company,' Aleksander said, throwing his hands in the air.

'No, you were trying to force him to go, using his company. You need to make him offer you his membership.'

'But how?'

She laughed at him then, a sound that hit him in the solar plexus. 'I can't do it *all* for you. *I'm* not a member of your secret cabal.'

'You have your own, remember?' he fired back, before realising that she was completely right. 'I have to go,' he said, getting up from the table and slipping into his suit jacket. He looked back in time to see the tease leaving her eyes, to be replaced by something else. It wasn't quite sadness, but it wasn't soft either.

'What is it?' he asked, his stomach clenching instinctively, preparing for a blow. She swallowed, the little flex of muscle at her jaw showing how much she was fighting whatever it was. 'You can tell me anything, Henna,' he replied truthfully.

She lifted her head and the look she gave him pierced something deep within him. 'I want more.'

Aleksander wasn't petty enough to pretend he didn't know what she was asking for. 'I can't give you that.'

'There's a difference between can't and won't.'

'Do you know what you're asking?' he demanded, angry that she was pushing him, making him want more than he could have.

'I'm asking for nothing more than the remaining days. But I'm asking for everything in them.'

'Everything?' he asked tonelessly. 'You are asking for the impossible. There is nothing more in me, Henna,' he said, turning from the table.

'I'm sorry,' she said, and he paused, half wanting to know why and half not. Unable to resist, he turned back to face her. 'I'm sorry that no one was there for you while you grieved. The way,' she said, her eyes glistening with unshed tears, 'that you were there for me.'

'I gave you nothing, Henna.'

'You gave me your hand, you gave me a friend, you gave me a family and a home. You gave me what I needed.'

It was a gut punch—that she knew what he'd wanted following Kristine's shocking decision devastated him. But she didn't understand that it was precisely not having that support that had made him who he was today. The king he was: accomplished, driven, single-minded…and broken. But, instead of admitting that to the smart, sexy woman sitting at his table, he turned and left the cabin.

Javier Casas was talking on his phone outside the hotel but terminated the call when he caught sight of Aleksander.

'You have an idea,' he correctly guessed when Aleksander came close enough.

'I do, but it's a risk.'

The Spaniard grinned, a light in his eyes, his arm thudding around Aleksander's shoulders. 'Since when did we play it safe?'

'We don't have much time.'

'Tell me.'

'Kozlov is all ego and would love nothing better than to best me, since I am why he lost his company. What if I gave him that chance?'

Javier's eyes narrowed in concentration. 'Go on.'

'He's in Macau right now,' Aleksander said, thankful for Gunnar's efficient intelligence-gathering. 'He's there for two days and then he's off. If we were to be in the same casino, what are the chances that he'd be so damn desperate to beat me at cards that he'd bet anything?'

'You think you can force him to put his membership as the ante?'

'Only if I offer him mine.'

Javier whistled. 'That *is* a risk. I'm not sure the others will like it.'

'They won't, and I don't have the time to talk them round.'

Javier grinned. 'You want me to do it.' After a brief consideration, he nodded in agreement. 'But,' he warned, 'you will owe me.'

'Fair enough,' Aleksander said, turning back to their cabin, his attention already on the fact that he and Henna would now be heading to Macau. Henna, who had been the key to solving the Kozlov problem. Henna, who had asked him for everything… and he had refused. Because in less than a week his future bride would be presented to the world…and it wasn't Henna.

# CHAPTER EIGHT

HENNA HAD TRAVELLED to many places with Freya over the last five years, but never in the King's plane. The aircraft had a shower, a bedroom that was as big as her suite and chair and table combinations that were cream leather and mahogany that screamed luxury.

She had taken the news about their new destination in resigned silence. She had stripped herself raw asking for more than he was prepared to give. But it had been her only chance to have the man she'd wanted from the first time she'd seen him. She could admit that to herself now. That all these years she had been hiding from the truth. Aleksander was far more than the older brother of her best friend, more than her employer, more than her King even.

Aleksander's awareness of her was as powerful as a touch. He might be staring intently at the emails she'd handled for him during his meetings in Öström, but she couldn't shake the feeling of it, the *weight*. She gratefully reached for the cup the air steward had brought her, the smell tingling her senses as she inhaled deeply and tiredly. Taking a sip, she sighed as the familiar flavours of bergamot and citrus hit her tongue. She let it soothe some of the tired hurt she felt pressing at the edges of her heart.

'It's good.' He nodded again, clearing his throat. 'Very good.'

She nodded, accepting his praise awkwardly. That was the problem. Since they'd left Öström—since he'd refused her request—they were out of step with each other again, even more so than since the Vårboll. It scratched at her skin and scrabbled back and forth across her stomach. It made her feel… She sighed and pressed her head back against the seat.

Things had shifted between them, of course they had. But she'd not been able to get her feet back on steady ground. She'd only made things worse.

'What are you drinking?' Aleksander asked, as if confused by the scent of her tea, an unusual type for Svardians.

She smiled, genuine warmth spreading through her as the memory rose in her mind. 'Earl Grey. It was my mother's favourite. My father told me that she was very specific about how the cup was made. Tea first, then milk.'

'No lemon?' he asked, familiar with the English tea.

'Though I'm sure there are those that would say she had it wrong, but she wouldn't have it any other way.'

'Is it okay for me to ask what your mother was like?'

Henna met his gaze, the look in his eyes one of someone who knew loss only as a deep wrenching pain. Her own was so different because of the way her father had shared her loss and grief, and his memories of her mother's joy and vibrant personality.

'Colourful. Every picture of her is full of intense bright colours,' she said, seeing the framed photographs she had taken from around the house and hidden in her bedroom before Viveca's mother arrived. 'My father met her in England, when he worked in his London office, and they fell in love. She didn't think twice about following him to Svardia. She passed away shortly after I was born from an aneurism, but my father would tell me something new about her every single day, even after he got sick. He made my feelings of loss for her something else. He turned it into curiosity and familiarity and warmth,' she said with a shrug. And when the echo of pain thudded in her chest for her father, she wrapped her arms around it and held onto the ache of her love tightly.

Aleksander was watching her intently in that way of his that made her feel seen. 'Who was there for you when you lost your father?'

*You.*

Henna shook the word from her mind, fighting her way back through her feelings to answer his question. 'My father had married Viveca's mother six months before he passed.' Henna knew her grief, accepted and cherished it even, but still the words were sometimes hard. 'He wanted someone to look after me when he was gone, and he and my mother had no other family. Marcella was a friend of his colleague and…she seemed nice,' Henna concluded.

'But she wasn't?'

'No.' She had stopped sugar-coating her experience with Viveca and her mother a long time ago. 'For the first year it didn't matter, because I was so shocked by my grief. I hadn't expected it. I thought… I thought that because I knew what it had felt like to not have my mother there, I…' She shrugged, even now chasing a breath because grief had filled her lungs. She desperately wished to comfort the utterly devastated child she'd been. 'But it shook me. And by the time I began to come back to the world around me everything had changed and they made it very clear that they didn't want me there,' she said simply.

Her home had become a place where every meal was painful and endured in silence from fear of making her stepmother even more frustrated with her or incurring the wrath of her stepsister. Where around every corner was absence and loss and reminders that her father was no longer there. Where every second felt as if she was a stranger and unwelcome in her own home. Was it any wonder that she had held on to the friendship Freya had offered with both hands and never let go? Any wonder that the Palace had been the truest home she'd had in years? A home that she was now about to leave.

'You will always have a place here,' he said, and

he was looking at her the way he'd first looked at her, when they'd met in the maze, and she wanted so much to believe him. To believe that what they'd shared the other night hadn't ruined everything.

Aleksander watched as Henna made her way to the bathroom, leaving a sense of sadness behind that seemed to fill the cabin. He couldn't imagine what it would be like to not feel safe in your place in the world. For him, he had been told over and over and over again until it was as sure as breathing, *You will be King.* His place in the world had always been, and would always be, a solid, certain thing. And he wasn't naïve about the fact that in taking this new job Henna was about to leave her sense of security behind…but he hated to think that she might have taken the role because she felt unwanted.

*Unwanted.*

The word teased and taunted. He didn't think that he'd ever wanted someone more. Ever. Mentally he was desperate to hold her to him, to pull her in and never let go, and emotionally he wanted her as far away as humanly possible. Because if he let her in… what would he let out?

The way Henna had described her grief, the shock, the numbness—he *knew* that feeling. He *knew* that pain. He'd never spoken about the loss of his unborn child, not even with his father, who had known of the pregnancy all along. Kristine had moved before he'd even had a chance to talk to her. To ask her if…if…

He clenched his jaw, fighting the questions that built in his mind, the anger, the hurt, the fear. The fear that it had been his fault from the very beginning, that it was his fault that he'd brought that pain down upon them and that Kristine had been forced into the most horrendous decision anyone could ever make. Emotion welled to the surface of his heart, drawing pinpricks of sweat across his spine and neck as he battled with the intensity of it.

His hands fisted on the armrests of the chair, knuckles white, fingers bruised red, until Henna's palm swept across the back of his hand and gently prised his fist open, because how could he hold on to such tension beneath such gentleness? He looked down to where she crouched beside his seat, her eyes not on his, but where she swept circles across his hands, her head bowed, and this time, rather than arousal, pure and simple, something complex wrapped around them, as warm as it was hot, as calming as it was urgent, as lasting as it was fleeting. In that moment Aleksander knew that, whatever it was, it was unique to her. Only to her. Only ever to her.

Apparently satisfied that he was no longer under the same ferocious hold of anger, she smoothed his now relaxed palm one last time and returned to her seat, turning her head into the crook of the cushion and closing her eyes.

'There's a bed,' he said, choosing to ignore what had passed between them.

'It's *your* bed, Your Majesty,' she replied, the title drawing a line between them that he was both angered by and thankful for.

He turned back to the laptop and stared at emails he couldn't see while he wrangled with the feelings that Henna brought to the surface and then swept away beneath her touch.

Twenty minutes later, Aleksander heard the slide of Henna's hair against the leather of the seat and tried to ignore it, but she had been restless in her sleep and every time she moved it drew his attention. The stubborn woman had refused to be comfortable and that it was fracturing his concentration was unacceptable.

The air steward had noticed and was about to approach to wake Henna, but Aleksander threw up a hand to ward him off. Henna had gone above and beyond in the last few days. As the staff member withdrew, Aleksander rubbed the tiredness from his eyes and stood, deciding that what he was about to do made practical sense and nothing more.

He rolled his shoulders before crossing the cabin and allowed himself one stolen minute just to look. Henna was about as watchful as he, so rarely had he got the chance to take her in. She really was exquisite. Beneath her fringe, long lashes swept downwards from her eyelids, curling and dark. Her skin was slightly flushed, but the thick dark brown ropes of her hair, shot through with gold, framed cheek-bones that were gentle but defined, as if everything in her was balanced between soft and strength, and he marvelled at it.

Her head turned again and her legs shifted. She clearly wasn't comfortable in that seat. He bent, slipping his hands to her back and beneath her legs, and gently pulled her into his arms. Instinctively she curled into his chest, her head resting against his shoulder as he turned towards the bedroom at the back of the plane. Of all the emotions he'd fought in the last few days, this was the most at peace he'd felt.

*Right. It feels right.*

Ignoring his inner thoughts, he carefully manoeuvred them into the bedroom and gently placed her down on the covers. Her body relaxed into the soft mattress, pinning his arms beneath her and bringing her chest to chest with him, the warm scent of her rising to tease his senses and beckon him over the line he'd placed between them. Shifting in his arms, her head turned towards his, their lips but a breath apart, and his heart leapt in his chest, pulse pounding like a drumbeat, impossible to ignore, urgent, needful and strong. Henna's eyes drifted open and he watched as the flare of surprise and desire obliterated the hazel ring to black. The sight of her reaction to him had need thickening his throat, a weight in his blood, hardening his arousal, and tension straining his muscles and just when he would have taken her lips in his she turned her head to the side, away from him.

A fist grabbed his gut and squeezed. He didn't have that right. He had refused her and now expected a kiss? He was a bastard and forced himself to see, to *know*, the hurt that she tried to hide. He closed his eyes and turned to go, but a hand sneaked out to grasp his wrist.

'You're tired and need to sleep too.'

'Henna, I—'

'Just sleep,' came her reply as she turned her head back to the pillow and closed her eyes.

Unable to deny her command, unable to fight the connection between them that had revealed itself, he toed off his shoes and, without breaking the hold she had on his wrist, lay down beside her, his body mirroring the curve of her back. There were mere inches between them, but Aleksander's last thought before being pulled into a deep sleep was that it might as well have been miles.

Henna stood by the window—another floor-to-ceiling reveal, but the view couldn't have been more different. Bright neon colours flashed and danced across skyscrapers which were mirrored in the sea below, bisected by the three bridges that connected Macau peninsula to Taipa and Coloane. From the seemingly impossible height of the hotel, Macau lay beyond her like a scattering of sequins on silk, the slightest ripple drawing her gaze to new and startlingly bright colours exploding across the cityscape. Her gaze feasted upon the sight, working so very hard to ignore the dress that Aleksander had procured for her.

She'd awoken on the plane's bed alone, but the warmth of the sheets beside her told her he'd only just risen. And she wondered if that was how it would always be between them now, her just a step behind, following in his footsteps. The thought had stung the backs of her eyes, before she'd pulled herself together and returned to the cabin, where the air steward had placed another Earl Grey tea beside her seat.

Typing away, Aleksander had barely spared her a glance as he'd informed her of the suite he'd booked for her and the clothing he'd arranged to be provided for her. Of all the things that had happened between them, it had been that which had angered Henna the most. She was well versed in last-minute change of plans, arranging clothing for Freya or Marit, suitable for any occasion, no matter where they were in the world. She was more than capable of providing for herself. So when she'd first seen the covered dress hanging on the back of the bedroom door, she had refused to look at it for at least twenty minutes. Until curiosity got the better of her and when she did…

Her heart had pounded. *Was this how he saw her?* Showered, and silky from the frangipani-scented body mousse that had left her skin feeling supple and smooth and worthy of the midnight-coloured creation, she stared at the dress, a boldness creeping over her skin and into her heart.

She held the spaghetti straps wide and slipped into the dress, sliding it up over her sensitive skin. The audaciously deep vee cut into the silk covering her chest took her breath away, the skirts parting high on her thigh as she walked closer to the mirror to inspect her reflection, and she drew her hand to her lips in shock. She turned, her entire back exposed but for the thin X of silk straps that held the dress in place, the blue silk gathering at the base of her spine scandalously.

Seeing herself like this, knowing that Aleksander had imagined her like this, she felt changed by it. The dress exposed as much as it concealed and the duality of it made her feel both sensual and beautiful, confident and powerful in a way she hadn't experienced before.

A message appeared on her phone, asking her to meet him at the bar of the hotel's casino. Her fingers flexed around the thin case.

*You are asking for the impossible. There is nothing more in me, Henna.*

She believed that he was wrong. But she'd asked. She'd asked and he'd refused her and she wasn't going to ask again.

Aleksander exited the private lift from his suite to the ground floor, frustrated that he'd been delayed by a call from Javier, confirming the organisation's agreement with his plan. That it gave him what he wanted was nothing compared to the fact that he'd made Henna wait.

The thought pulled him up midstride and he paused, his hand reaching towards his temples and lowering again before betraying such an obvious sign of frustration. The realisation of just how important she had become to him had him almost turning on his heel. Until he caught sight of a flash of blue silk. Fists flexing and heart pounding, he took one step and then another, enthralled by the siren's call of her exposed skin and the need to feel it, anywhere against him and any *way*. He watched as the barman placed a martini glass on the marble top in front of Henna and in the reflection of the mirrored glass behind the bar she caught his gaze.

A hundred little explosions shattered his equilibrium to the point where he was genuinely surprised the entire bank of bottles containing some of the world's most expensive alcohol hadn't collapsed and smashed to the floor. Shards of jade scattered across Henna's irises before she blinked them away and lifted the glass to her lips without breaking their connection.

He felt his own pupils widen in response to the power of her gaze. There was neither challenge nor submission in it—simply a recognition of self-worth and it made her devastating. The acute awareness of the impact she had on him was to the point of near pain as the physical and emotional threatened to coalesce. Her lips opened just slightly—as if perhaps she was about to say something—when Aleksander became aware of a figure approaching from his left.

Marshalling himself with a ruthlessness honed from years of practice, he turned to greet the short, stocky suited man and his extremely tall companion. Aware of the attention they were drawing, Aleksander was conscious that it was unusual for two members of the organisation to greet each other so openly, but then again Kozlov had just sold his shares in the company he'd built from the ground up because Aleksander and Lykos had been able to obtain controlling shares. It would be best to remember that Kozlov was a man who would cut off his nose to spite his face. It made him dangerous. It also made the Russian very angry.

'Your Majesty,' Kozlov greeted him with a considerable amount of venom.

In response, Aleksander inclined his head, his features masking his own fury. Looking closely, he could see the suspicion beneath the anger simmering in the Russian's gaze.

'What are you doing here?' the oligarch demanded and Aleksander couldn't work out if it was the man's stupidity or intolerable arrogance that made him feel he could address royalty in such a way.

'I heard that the Sultan of Bur'hran was here and I plan to relieve him of his favourite thoroughbreds, so if you'll excuse me,' Aleksander said, making to walk away.

'What, you do not wish to try your hand against me again?' The jeer in Kozlov's tone was music to Aleksander's ears, slowing his steps and turning him back. 'Worried you might lose this time?'

'You have nothing left that interests me, Kozlov,' Aleksander dismissed.

For a moment the mask slipped on the face of the statuesque blonde on the Russian's arm, her eyes widening in shock, before Kozlov yanked her back into place on his arm. The move nearly pulled the woman off her feet and Aleksander's hackles rose with the need to wipe the sneer off the billionaire's face. He should never have been permitted as a member of the organisation. The organisation should be there to protect others from people like this.

'But you have something *I* want,' Kozlov snapped. His tone grated against Aleksander's nerves, but the way he ignored the evident discomfort of the woman beside him was unconscionable.

'Spit it out or hold it in, Kozlov. You're wasting my time,' Aleksander said, not bothering to hide his disdain.

Ilian glared at him, the man's cheeks going an unhealthy shade of red.

'I want a seat at the table. The *top* table.'

Aleksander's smile was lethal. 'No.' He walked off, his pulse racing in his chest, counting the footsteps that took him further and further away from the Russian. *One, two, three—*

'I'll play you for it. If you win, I will give up my membership. If I win, I will take yours.'

The thrill that went through Aleksander was like lightning. He turned back, making his response seem behind disbelief. 'Without complaint? I don't trust you, Kozlov.'

'We can draw up an agreement in advance. The house will witness and hold the ante.' Such agreements were ill advised and irregular, but not unheard of and exactly what Aleksander had hoped for. All the sweeter that Kozlov believed it was his idea. Desperation practically dripped from the man. A desperation that was all too familiar to Aleksander.

Consenting to the wager Kozlov thought was his, they went through the requirements with the casino's concierge and Aleksander realised that there had been a time in his life when things could have been very different for him. Publicly, he had never put a foot wrong, he'd never come off the rails, missed an exam, received anything less than a merit in school and college. But privately, he had skated very close to a very thin edge. Alcohol and gambling had been within easy reach of a very rich royal who was happy to roll the dice between the temptation of oblivion and the pressure of a role that had cost him the girl he'd loved and a child he'd desperately wanted. Because he *had* always wanted children. Whether because it was required of him and the role he was born to play, or whether it was innate within him, it hadn't mattered.

But when that possibility had been taken away from him it had shattered that softer, happy, carefree part of him. Until he'd played a single hand of cards with the man who would become his mentor. Aleksander honestly couldn't have said what the older man had seen in him, but he'd be eternally thankful that he'd been pulled back from the brink of disaster before he could ruin his life irrevocably. Aleksander had lost that innocent part of him, but he had been stopped from embracing the darkness completely.

But even now, sitting at the private poker table away from the murmur of conversation and voices placing bets and bemoaning losses, Aleksander felt that same sweep of recklessness pulling at him. Half of his attention was back at the bar where he'd left Henna twenty minutes ago. He would give her any number of apologies she needed, but Kozlov had to be handled now.

He lifted the tips of his two cards and looked at the four in the centre of the table. He'd played Kozlov enough times that they didn't need to feel each other out. Although he often seemed erratic, there was a blunt driving force behind the way the oligarch played his hands. He quickly assessed the Russian's chips—he was down against Aleksander, but that could change in a hand or two. Even then, he decided to let go of this hand and folded.

Kozlov swept up the chips on the table and ordered a vodka. Aleksander checked his watch before the waiter turned to him, distracting Aleksander from the approach of the concierge.

'Gentlemen, we have another player. This is amenable to you?'

Another player was the last thing Aleksander wanted, but when he caught the look in Kozlov's gaze he wondered whether it might present a distraction for the Russian.

'Our deal would not change?' he asked.

'The winner retains the loser's membership,' Kozlov confirmed, his gaze flicking between Aleksander, the concierge and the third player.

'And the new player?' he demanded, unwilling to break eye contact with the Russian.

'Plays only what's on the table,' Kozlov replied, meaning they wouldn't have to offer an equal stake to the agreement regarding the membership. After a quick calculation Aleksander agreed. It wasn't as if this new player would pose any kind of threat, he was confident in his skills.

The thought burned to dust when he saw the player take their seat. He snapped his jaw shut before an expletive could escape and betray him. With a buy-in of five hundred thousand he couldn't fathom how Henna had made it to the private table.

# CHAPTER NINE

SHE WAS BLAMING her audacity on the dress. *And* that she only had a short time left in Aleksander's employ. *And* the fact that she hated the idea of him confronting Kozlov alone. He'd explained enough about the man for her to not want Aleksander anywhere near him and she hadn't liked the look of the bodyguards the Russian had placed either side of the entrance to the private tables. It was unexplainable and, probably for Aleksander, inexcusable, but Henna simply knew that she had to be in here.

'Kozlov,' the Russian said by way of introduction.

'Olin,' she replied in kind. The oligarch narrowed his eyes and she could have sworn she felt Aleksander still dangerously, as if he were watching every single move.

'As in Technologies?' Kozlov asked.

Henna inclined her head in acknowledgement, even though Olin Tech was no longer owned by her family.

'I met your father once. He was...ferociously intelligent.'

'He was,' she said, refusing to let her dislike for the Russian colour her reply. Even had Aleksander not told her about the man, he made her skin crawl, though she couldn't have said why. While Kozlov's attention was on her, Aleksander's fury was clear in his eyes, but the moment the Russian returned his gaze to the table it was masked.

'Your Highness,' she addressed him.

'You two know each other?' the heavily accented question split the table.

'Everyone knows the King of Svardia,' she dismissed easily. She was aware that Aleksander thought her in need of protection, but she'd meant what she said back in Öström: *she* knew bullies. She also knew cards. At first when she'd been very young, her father had taught her how to count quickly, with a simple game. He would turn over a series of cards and she would have to add them up. Then he taught her games like whist, and rummy, and vingt-et-un, and when he'd been stuck in the hospital they would play poker. It had been her father's favourite and had quickly become hers.

'The ante is ten thousand,' Aleksander warned, and she inclined her head, realising that he had no idea of her financial situation. It might have seemed strange to some that Henna would continue to work whilst she had a not so small fortune in her bank account. Her father had been a billionaire in his own right and while he'd married Marcella and given her the estate and a monthly income upon his death,

Henna had received the larger part of his considerable wealth.

Henna placed her chips on the table, realising that she enjoyed surprising Aleksander. He, who seemed to know all and see all. It made her proud—as if she'd accomplished something that very few people did.

The dealer looked to each of them and started to deal. The first few hands were played in silence, each of the players getting used to the new dynamic. Henna surfed the rise and fall in her adrenaline levels and the mental agility required to mask her responses from two intelligent and very different opponents, while looking for tells that would betray their cards. Occasionally the statuesque blonde would appear at Kozlov's side, pout and require some money before she disappeared, but for the most part the focus was on the hands.

She'd just folded a mediocre hand when Kozlov said, 'I don't think you have played here before, Miss Olin. I'm sure that I would have recognised you.'

She locked her gaze with the Russian's, rather than meet Aleksander's piercing glare.

'It has been some time since I played,' she admitted, while feigning interest in a possible pair.

'Well, I have had the pleasure of playing the King of Svardia quite recently, and I must admit he won a considerable stake from me. I have not forgiven him.'

'If you lost your hand, Mr Kozlov, the fault lies not with him.'

'My intent is simply to warn you that he often has another agenda,' replied the Russian, his gaze boring into hers. 'He's always thinking two steps ahead.'

Henna willed everything in her not to tense, the way her stomach had. She couldn't give the game away. But there was something in his warning, something that she felt she should not so easily disregard.

'Stop pontificating, Kozlov, and play your hand,' Aleksander growled, glaring at Kozlov.

Kozlov threw another ten thousand into the pot without taking his eyes from Henna. 'He has no patience,' he mocked.

That Kozlov was taunting Aleksander was unsurprising to Henna. That he was using her was either spite or he somehow knew that Henna worked for the royal family. The bet was to her and she chose to raise, drawing a glimmer of attention from both men, before the dealer revealed the turn.

'I find honesty is the best way to play,' she said, this time looking straight into Aleksander's stormy glare and refusing to bow to the power of that tempest. She felt the words like a spell casting them both to hell—hot, fiery and delicious until they burned whatever this madness was between them.

The fourth card in the centre of the table got her close to the hand she wanted, but she would have to wait to see how the men chose to bet. Her heart was thumping, adrenaline coursing through her veins, and she wrestled her body under control, determined not to betray her feelings.

'Honesty. How novel,' remarked the Russian, as if amused by such an idea. 'Aleksander? What are your thoughts on honesty?'

'Final bets,' the dealer announced into the brief moment of silence.

Aleksander pushed three hundred thousand onto the table. 'My thoughts are simple, Kozlov. You threatened my sister. My intention is to make you pay for that for a *very* long time.'

Henna's gaze flashed between the two men, surprised that Aleksander would reveal such a thing. Kozlov met the three hundred thousand on the table.

'Well, I suppose that depends on who wins, doesn't it? he sneered, dripping arrogance and venom in equal measure. If either man noticed that she added her bet to the pot she couldn't say, prompting the unflappable dealer to reveal the fifth and final card.

Everything in Henna stopped—her heart, her breath, her blood. The men were still staring each other down but all she could see was the one card she'd needed.

The King of Hearts.

'Well, Your Majesty? Can you beat this?' the Russian growled as he threw down a straight.

White noise filled Aleksander's ears, his eyes almost seeing stars from the adrenaline coursing through his veins. He wasn't looking at Kozlov's hand, though, but Henna—her eyes bright, round and impossible to read. Her skin glowed against the indigo silk of the dress, the deep vee he wanted to slip his fingers beneath, the flicker of her pulse at her throat that he wanted to taste. In an instant, his thirst for vengeance was quashed and all he wanted was her. To give her what she'd asked for—*everything*.

Aleksander tossed his cards across the table, revealing the flush that beat Kozlov's hand. 'Your membership is mine,' Aleksander said, pushing back from the table, impatient to get Henna away from the oligarch and alone in his suite.

'And your money is *mine*,' said Henna, looking at the Russian as she stood, her eyes blazing with victory.

'Four of a kind,' the dealer observed, yanking both Aleksander and Kozlov's gazes to Henna's hand. 'Miss Olin wins,' he said, pushing the chips towards Henna. Aleksander's heart pumped fiercely in his chest, pride, power, awe, delight filling his body until he felt fit to burst. Henna slid a chip to the dealer and her considerable winnings were taken care of by the concierge, who slipped away discreetly.

'You were both in on it? You cheated!' Kozlov yelled.

The dealer signalled to Security.

'One should not question the integrity of the King, nor the casino in their ability to spot a cheat, Kozlov,' Aleksander warned as suited men appeared, already flanking Kozlov's bodyguards.

'Nor should one underestimate the women of

Svardia,' Henna added. 'You will stay away from Marit, from our country *and* from the organisation,' she commanded.

Kozlov's mouth opened and closed wordlessly, until a fierce purple bruised his cheeks. Aleksander skirted the table to meet Henna, his palm pressing gently against the bare skin at the base of her spine, sending an electrical firestorm through his body and, without a single glance back at the Russian, together they left the private tables.

In silence, Aleksander ushered her through the public tables of the casino, passed the bar where he'd first seen her and across the black and white marble floored foyer to the private elevator, beyond the main bank of elevators. The heat of her skin taunted him, burned him as they waited for the gold doors to the penthouse suite's elevator to open. He shifted so that he stood behind her, his chest to her back, giving him access to her neck and the sensitive place he knew would drive her wild, just beneath her ear. It certainly drove him wild.

His heart pounded as it worked to force blood around his body, sluggish with desire and want.

'Before, you asked me for everything. Is that still what you want?' he demanded, his voice dark with a lust he could leash only if she commanded it.

'Yes,' she said, meeting his gaze in the mirrored reflection of the elevator doors.

'Even though it will never be more?' he warned.

'If you give me everything tonight, it will be enough,' she assured him.

And even though he knew it was a lie—because it would never be enough for him—he allowed it because his need for her was now too great to be stopped unless she commanded it.

The elevator doors opened and he ushered her forward, keeping her back to his chest. The rise and fall of her chest drew his gaze, his fingers instinctively grasping her at the hip and pulling her back against his body, against the clear evidence of how much he wanted her. As the doors closed behind them, desire pulled and pushed at him, ebbing between his possessive need for her and his instinct to reprimand her. He had hated that she had been near Kozlov but he rejoiced in her triumph and besting them both at cards.

'When did you learn to play poker?' he whispered as the thumb of his free hand came up to caress her shoulder blade. Her skin pebbled as his breath rolled over it, his lips barely an inch from the curve of her neck. Consciously or not, she had bent her head to give him better access. Her nipples pressed points against the midnight silk of her dress.

Her silence drew his gaze to her reflection in the mirrored walls. 'Before you, I'd imagine,' she teased. This bold Henna, this powerful, sensual creature, was his for the night and there would be no holding back. She deserved what she'd asked for. Not because she had beaten both him and Kozlov, but because of who she was. Because she was more regal and more worthy than anyone he'd ever met. He raised an eyebrow and she bit her tongue, little tremors beginning to filter through her body, but her gaze was steady, the look a challenge, a dare.

'Everything,' she replied to the question he'd been about to voice, as her arm swept up so that her hand could reach his neck, her fingers tangling in the hair above his nape. The gesture pressed her breasts forward and his hands itched to cup them, to feel the delicate weight of them in his palm. He read the truth in her eyes, the fire and heat of her need for him, and could no longer deny her a single thing.

He smoothed the silk straps from her shoulders and the dress dropped from her body like a magician's reveal. Her gasp was drowned out by the ferocious pounding of his heart. He covered her breasts with his arm, pulling her against him, and she shifted against his arousal, her back arching her breasts against his forearm. He was wearing too many clothes, while Henna was in nothing but a midnight-coloured thong and high heels.

Her body was on fire, branded by Aleksander's touch, by the scorching heat of his gaze, and it was glorious. Every single touch, every single lick, kiss, bite, she felt it all over her body. It was shameless and she didn't care. Her head fell back against his shoulder and he devoured her neck with open-mouthed kisses and growls of need that arrowed to her pulsing core.

The door to the elevator opened behind them, the swooshing sound audible until she let out a delicate cry as he swept her off her feet and into his arms. Her arms instinctively looped around his neck as her shoes fell to the floor, her hands interlocking and her gaze fastened to his. The thread of humour that had begun from embarrassment at the sound of her surprise evaporated beneath the heat of his scrutiny.

He stalked through the penthouse suite and came into a room bathed in an array of colours: fuchsia, ice-blue, rich gold, lush green and effervescent purple. He laid her on the bed beneath a kaleidoscope of city lights through the window and he was still the most glorious sight she'd ever seen.

He shucked the tux jacket from his shoulders and tossed it aside. He yanked the bow tie from his throat, snapping one end free and sliding it from round his neck. She backed up on the bed as his eyes stalked over her, devouring her without laying a finger on her.

'You are my weakness—do you know that?' he asked as his hands pulled the shirt from his trousers, and all she could do was watch. His words were fire through the ice in her veins, heating her from deep within. His movements were efficient, impatient even, and there shouldn't have been anything erotic about the sharp, tension-filled actions that undid buttons, but there was.

'You could ask for anything right now and I would give it. Do you understand?' he demanded furiously, as he tore the shirt from his shoulders and threw it across the room. His anger only fuelled her desire. Because she was angry too. Angry that he could never be hers. Angry because she suddenly understood why. 'I have spent years ensuring that no one would ever get close enough to betray me again. But you? You wouldn't have to. You could take everything from me and I'd still want to give you more.'

She saw it then—how vulnerable he thought she made him, how weak. She saw his thinking as if it were being written in the air between them. He had been made to pay the ultimate price in order to rule, and to make it worth it, to make *Kristine's decision* worth it, he had to be the best ruler—no weakness, no vulnerability, no emotion. She wished she could show him that there was another way to be, another way of living that didn't involve him cutting himself off from everyone around him. But he was clinging so desperately to the belief that had enabled him to survive his grief, the belief that cutting off all emotion was the only way forward, that she didn't dare take it from him. Tears gathered in her eyes as she nodded. 'I understand.'

'Henna, I—'

He shook his head, cutting off whatever it was he would have said, kneeled on the bed and pulled her into a kiss that stole as much as it gave, that thrilled as much as it drugged, that soothed even as it broke her into a thousand pieces.

His lips opened hers, worshipping her, breathing life into the far reaches of her desires, of her sense of self, and she couldn't explain how much she wanted him, how much she needed him. She reached for the button of his trousers, pulling back to see his eyes glazed with a heady need. She palmed the length of his erection, the solid heat of his arousal just for her. He caught her wrist, stopping her when she pulled at the zip.

'You said I could have everything tonight,' she whispered, her desire to taste him as he had tasted her so strong it had become a mantra. Admitting it painted her cheeks with a blush that stung, and she feared he might refuse her, until he cursed and let go of her wrist.

She slid the zip down and ran the pad of her thumb delicately over the soft dull pink head of his penis where it crested the band of his briefs. His body shivered beneath her touch and she marvelled at such clear evidence of how she affected him. She swept the briefs down over his erection and hips, freeing him, and he shifted so that she could slip them from his legs.

Turning and lying back against the silk bedding, Aleksander watched her, his gaze revealing the sheer intensity of his anticipation. Sliding between his thighs and lowering, she licked slowly up the length of his hardened erection as it jerked against her tongue, the power, the heat and the dusky taste of him all for her. As she took him into her mouth, his hips bucked lightly and she clasped the base of his shaft, pushing down gently, delighted when his hips bucked again and a curse fell from his lips.

Slick and salty on her tongue, his thighs tense and corded beneath her touch, she felt the power of having Aleksander trembling beneath her, mindless with pleasure *she* had brought him, and surprised by the pleasure she brought herself. Her tongue swept a caress across the head of him and this time Aleksander reached for her with both hands. 'If I have only one night with you, Henna, do not make me wait,' he said, staring down at her, his eyes ablaze.

He pulled her up the length of his body and kissed her with an intensity that seared her soul, that teased already taut nipples and pulsed an over-sensitised core, before he rolled her beneath him.

Braced on one arm, his hand swept down her body, his fingers hooking beneath the thin band at her hip and sliding the thong down her legs and from her feet. He clasped her calf, his fingers travelling up over her knee and thigh to luxuriate in the soft crosshatch of curls. Restless, her legs shifted against his thighs, wanting more and more from his touch, and when he finally parted her to his scrutiny, rather than feel exposed, the raw ferocity in his gaze made her feel powerful, wanted, *needed.* He cupped her, pressing the heel of his palm against her clitoris and teasing her with two thrusting fingers.

He was brutal in his determination to drown her in as much pleasure as he could and, unlike last time, her orgasm built with a decadent inevitability, first sweeping at her feet like the tide, then rising inch by delicious inch through her body, warming her skin with tingles and dusting it with a pink flush. Her thighs quivered as it passed, it tripped over her ribs and flooded her lungs, making her gasp for air, it filled her throat and rolled her eyes and, when it finally hit, her body arched the wave and her soul soared into the midnight sky.

'Aleksander.'

His name was a sob on her lips and he'd seen every single second of her pleasure and it had humbled him. He couldn't stop touching her. His palms stroked her thighs, her hip, waist, anything he could touch, because for this night only she was his. He marvelled at her skin, pebbling beneath his palm, flushing beneath his gaze, dotted with golden freckles and dark moles that were a constellation he wanted to trace each night until he had mapped her, until she was *known*.

The thought was enough to scare him. Her eyes found his, as if she had sensed the change in him. He smiled away her concern as he pressed the feeling down deep within him and bent to kiss her shoulder, her neck, and beneath his lips she arched against him.

'Henna—'

'Please, Aleksander.'

Her whispered words tore at his heart.

'Even with a condom—' he began, hating that the thought of duty and the whisper of grief had entered their bed and become stuck in his throat.

'I am also on the contraceptive pill,' she explained, holding his gaze with compassion, understanding and so much more than he deserved. It was as safe as it could ever be, and it was still the most dangerous thing he could ever do. 'But I would never ask you to do something you didn't want to do,' she said solemnly.

He huffed out a grim laugh. He wanted her more than he had ever wanted anyone. For so many years he had kept so much to himself, bottled up, fizzing beneath the lid, and finally he felt understood by her and it was the absolute worst thing that she could do. Because she would know that it was his carelessness that had cost him and Kristine so much, even if they had only been teenagers.

But he wasn't a teenager now, and neither was Henna. They were as protected as they could be. The slide of her thigh against the outside of his calf started a silky friction that quickly incited a firestorm of need. He couldn't change the way he was, the way he'd made himself twelve years ago, but he could give Henna what she wanted tonight.

He reached for the bedside table drawer and withdrew a condom, her heavy-lidded gaze steadfastly on his as he tore the foil wrapper and drew the latex over the length of his erection. Turning back, he braced himself on forearms that bracketed a face he would hold in his heart until he could no longer remember anything else.

She parted her legs for him and just before he entered her, just before he pushed into the softest heat he'd ever known, his last thought before need became a crashing urgent thing was that he felt safe. But the smooth, slow slide robbed him of all thought, leaving him capable only of the growl that left his lips, met and matched by Henna's gentle moan, as if they both finally crossed an invisible threshold that they'd fought against for too long.

A part of Aleksander wanted to lie there, luxuriating in the silken muscles that gripped him more intimately than he'd ever felt before, but the raw animal part of him wanted more. He withdrew, pulling a whimpered protest from Henna, urging him back into her deeper and faster, and the sigh of satisfaction that met his every thrust was all he needed. Again and again, he drove them to the brink of her orgasm, and again and again, he pulled her back with gentle hands, telling himself that it was for Henna, that he wanted to bring her what she deserved.

It wasn't a lie, but it also hid a truth. That, buried deep within her, was the closest thing to complete he'd ever felt and he wasn't ready to let it go.

He luxuriated in the feeling, drawing it out until he thought that he might be able to take it with him for the rest of his life. And finally, when their bodies were sweat-soaked and fevered, when the pleas from her lips met the desperation in his chest, when his body trembled with the effort of holding back and could no longer fight, he thrust them into an abyss of such infinite pleasure he wasn't sure he even wanted to find his way back.

# CHAPTER TEN

ALEKSANDER WAS STILL sleeping when Henna quietly padded back into the room after her shower. She pulled the soft robe tighter around her shoulders as if to protect herself from the impact of the sight of the King of Svardia sprawled across the bed, the sheet draped across his abdomen *just about* protecting his modesty.

The thought drew a smile to her lips, then a warmth to her cheeks as she remembered that he had absolutely nothing to be modest about. Before they had fallen into an exhausted sleep, Aleksander had stayed true to his word and given her everything she could possibly have desired from a night with him. He had lavished her with pleasure and she had come apart beneath the ruthlessness of his focus. Even now a pulse between her legs flared to life and just for a moment she thought she could feel him again. There had been times when he had moved so deeply within her that the lines had blurred between them, as if they had become one and…and…

Her heart stuttered. She had felt as if she had found a part of herself she'd never known she missed. As if she might never be lonely ever again.

The ground suddenly felt unsteady beneath her feet and her heart began to shake in her chest. She loved him. She *loved* him. Complex and infuriating, but always with a core of unshakable integrity, he was a king who loved his country and a billionaire determined to make the world better in secret, a man who had compassion for her grief and no patience for his own. He was resolute in his convictions, ambitious and determined, but when the reins slipped he could be funny and charming, surprising and desperately sexy. Aleksander wasn't easy, but his care for those he considered his was fierce. And she *knew* he cared for her. But he saw her as a threat to his country and to him—that was unacceptable and nothing she could say or do would change his mind.

Silencing the sob on her lips, she turned to the window but for the first time couldn't see beyond the glass. Instead, she saw their return to Svardia, her office, welcoming Freya back, completing the final arrangements for her engagement party, travelling to London and all the little things that would be her future without Aleksander. From the moment they left this room she would never feel the heat of his body against hers, his lips against her skin, she would never feel warmed by the connection between them that had felt so pure and so private.

Her heart began to pound in her chest, her breath

coming a little quicker, a cold sheen gathering at her nape, making her shiver, tremble in some awful contrast to how she had shaken in his arms. She was grieving for a loss she had refused to consider before, but now it demanded recognition, demanded to be heard. She loved him but she could never have him because he had closed himself off from anything that would remotely engage him emotionally. He had imprisoned himself within a maze so convoluted and complex, designed in grief and duty, that her heart just broke for him. Tears pressed at the corners of her eyes and her arms, wrapped tight around her ribs, were the only things holding her from falling apart.

A movement in the reflection of the window caught her eye. Aleksander was behind her, the white sheet wrapped around his waist, his body full of the kind of push-pull tension she'd begun to recognise in him when he wanted something but wouldn't let himself have it—and it broke her heart that it was her.

'Do you regret it?' Aleksander winced as the words raked his throat raw. Everything he wanted to say but couldn't was trying to get out, fighting tooth and nail. It was a question that he'd never had the chance to ask Kristine, but he wouldn't shy away from the truth this time. Henna deserved more than his cowardice. Everything in him braced for the words that would send him to a hell of his own making. His hands were fisted, jaw clenched, thighs rock hard, holding him in place. He didn't think he'd be able to bear it if—

'No, Aleksander,' she said, turning. The sincerity written across her face wasn't even enough to break the hold that fear had on him. Her hand came up to the side of his face and he turned into her palm, seeking a solace he didn't deserve. Warmth spread from her skin to his body, pushing back the cold darkness that had threatened to overwhelm him.

'No,' she said again, as if knowing he needed to hear it. Then she pressed her lips to his, once, twice, and a third time. Gentle brushes, slowly teasing his mouth open beneath her caress, and when he gave in it felt like his victory, not hers. Drawn into the sensual dance as if hypnotised by her touch, he pulled at the thin tie holding the robe together and slipped his hands beneath the silk to find the glory of her skin.

His hand swept around her waist and pulled her fiercely against his body and not once did she break the kiss or protest, even though they both knew she should. He lifted her up, bracing her with one arm as her legs wrapped around his hips, and he drew the silk away from her body and threw the sheet from his waist, bringing them skin to skin in a way that had them both trembling in seconds.

She fitted against him as if she'd been made to be there and everything in him roared against the restraint that pulled him back from simply plunging deep within her, seduced by the need to slide skin to skin with no barrier between them. Need was a war cry in his mind, but one he would never give in to.

He took them to the bed, aware of just how little it had taken for them to go from caress to carnal and the look in her lust-filled gaze appeared dazed by the same thought. 'I can—'

'Finish what you started, Your Majesty,' she interrupted, the challenge, the tease, the desire so clear beneath the command she had uttered, he delighted in it and determined to do just as she had asked.

'Henna?'

She turned to see Lisbeth coming down the corridor towards her. She smiled at the young woman she had worked with for three years, who would—happily—be taking over as Freya's lady-in-waiting after Henna left. And then her smile turned into a frown when she saw the first look of concern mar Lisbeth's features since accepting her promotion.

'Is everything okay?' Immediately her thoughts flew to Freya, then Marit, and finally her heart stopped altogether when she thought of something happening to—

'Yes, yes.' She nodded, a little frantically. Henna had never seen her so unsettled, and it wouldn't bode well for her future if she didn't get that under control. 'I just… Are you going to your office?'

'Yes, I left some paperwork there.'

'Right, only…'

Henna heard her office door open behind her and

turned to find Freya, leaning half out of it. 'Ah, there you are. Can you…?' She beckoned Henna forward.

Had Freya been looking for her? As promised, when she and Kjell had returned from their break, the two friends had spent an entire day together, no work, just catching up. It had been wonderful and Freya's newfound happiness was glorious to see.

*But what about you? You deserve your happiness.*

Her father's voice had whispered into her mind as she'd laughed and smiled with her closest friend. Twice Freya had asked if she were okay. Both times, she'd been thinking of Aleksander and both times she'd lied and said she was fine.

She had thought it would stop when they returned to Svardia—the strange sense that she knew where he was. It was a kind of foresight that warned her when he was near, raising the hair on her arms and neck, her pulse suddenly beginning to spin out of rhythm. Unable to marshal the reaction she had to him, it was as if he owned her, body and soul. The battle between fire and ice raging across her body made a part of her long for the end of her notice period but the other cling on desperately, hoping against all odds that he might change his mind.

And then she realised how foolish that was. As if he, King of Svardia, would pick *her*. That voice sounded horribly like Viveca's, but she couldn't shake it off. Henna had told him the truth in Macau. She didn't regret spending that one night with him. If that was all she would ever have, she would keep it with her for the rest of her life. But she wished she'd known beforehand just how much it would *hurt*.

'Come on.' Freya hurried just as Henna's feet grew heavier. Despite Freya's and Lisbeth's now palpable excitement, Henna was certain that Aleksander was in her office. Determining to relax, Henna let the two pull her into her office, where—

'Surprise!' a chorus of voices shouted out.

Her little office was packed full of people—so many that they were overflowing into the adjacent office through the open connected door. A banner had been hung across her desk and paper streamers thrown about, little plates of food were being shared and when a glass was thrust into her hand by Freya and she found herself pushed back into a chair in the centre of the room she couldn't help but allow a wobbly smile to pull at her lips.

'You thought we'd just let you go without throwing you a goodbye party?' Freya teased.

'Well, I thought that most of you would be preparing for *someone else's* party,' she teased. Most of the staff members groaned and then laughed when Freya said, 'Hey, I haven't been that bad!'

This was what Henna loved about working at the Palace. It wasn't the prestige. It wasn't the access to some of the world's most influential people. It was the family that they had created. The work was long hours, intense and incredibly locked down due to the sensitive information they had access to. But the core staff, they were more than friends, and Henna realised for the first time that it wasn't just Freya and Marit and their brother she would be leaving. It was Anita Bergqvist, who had been one of the first people to congratulate her, it was Jean and Ella from Admin, it was Mikael, Anders and Birgit from Security, it was all the people who had come together today, happy for her, and sad to see her go.

'No, *you* haven't been that bad,' someone groused, clearly thinking of how difficult Aleksander had been recently.

'I heard that,' said a voice from the back of the room.

While good-humoured apologies were given, the soft centre of Henna's core began to shake a little and goosebumps raised on her skin. Not that anyone would have noticed—she had become expert at hiding her reaction to Aleksander.

'Speech! Speech!'

She let out a purposely audible groan. 'No, no,' she said, shaking her head, but the cries were insistent. She looked around at the sea of faces, all bright-eyed and so thrilled for her. She felt the heat of Aleksander's focus on her back, torn between being pleased that he'd come and sad at the distance between them.

'Not many people know what we do,' she began, 'which is, admittedly, the *point* of what we do,' she stressed to their laughter, 'but it *is* important. Important that the people of Svardia have faith in our…our family.' She looked to Freya, her heart warm with love for a woman more sister than friend. 'Faith in our Princesses and our King,' she said, angling her head to the side, acknowledging him but unable to meet the gaze she felt burning into her skin. 'Often this requires sacrifice, and almost always that sacrifice is unseen, and unknown. But *we* know. *We* see. We understand and we...thank you for it,' she said, her words shivering with emotion.

Although tears glistened in Freya's eyes and many of her colleagues', she knew that Aleksander had heard her words, her message to him. She wanted him, *needed* him, to know that, no matter how much it hurt, she understood. Understood the sacrifice that had been made for him in the past and the one he was making now, so that Svardia would have the incredible King that he would be.

'We're supposed to be thanking you!' cried Freya, pulling her into a fierce hug that Henna honestly needed in that moment. Especially when she felt the King slip from the room in the middle of the fuss. And even though she shouldn't, even though she knew it was wrong, she excused herself for a moment and hurried into the corridor.

The sound of the door opening stopped Aleksander mid-stride. He pulled up short, his pulse pounding in his chest. He was too close to a line he wanted to burn. He didn't want to let her go.

Even though he shouldn't, he couldn't not turn. He *had* to see her. Because he knew that once she left, that would be it. There would be no more teasing, no more understanding. There would be no more gentle smiles easing into pleasure-filled sighs. There would be no more shivers to soothe beneath the palm of his hand. He would return to a world where he kept secrets and trust behind locked doors. So right now, here, he would take in as much as he could of her. Slowly, his body moving from his heart not his head, he turned, and immediately wished he hadn't.

She was so utterly beautiful and she had no earthly idea of it. Her eyes gleamed with a knowing sorrow, but she wasn't cowed by it. It had made her strong, stronger than he ever would be, he thought as, step by step, they closed the distance between them until he felt the heat of her through their clothes and there was but an inch between them.

There were so many things he wanted to say, but nothing came to his lips. Instead, his eyes ravished her features, committing them to a memory he was already pushing deep within him. He teetered on the brink, fighting himself and the roaring in his ears that demanded he kiss her, pull her to him and never let go. But he couldn't. He just couldn't risk it. He would burn it all down for her if she asked him to, and what would that make of him as a man? As a king? What would that make of the sacrifice Kristine had made so that he could be the King Svardia needed? It would make it worthless and he could *never* allow that.

He felt her gaze across his face, as if she too was

taking this moment, memorising it, locking it away for some unimaginable future apart. His heart ached even as it was soothed by her presence and in that silent shared moment he passed through every possible feeling. He shared it with her in the silence as it couldn't be shared out loud, he shared and took until there was nothing left. Because he was her King and she was the only woman he could never marry, for the simple reason that she was too much of a threat to him.

Something shattered in him then. He felt it, an actual loss deep within him. Henna took the smallest step back, as if she'd realised it too. He'd been about to follow, to reach out for her like the drowning man he was, when the door to her office opened and Freya emerged into the corridor.

Aleksander pulled back but it was too late. He knew his sister had seen too much, even without taking his eyes from the woman in front of him.

'Henna, is everything okay?'

It said something that his sister's first thought was for Henna.

This was it, he knew. The last time that he would see her as she was. The last time he would let himself near her without the barriers his heart was already looking to hide behind. He drank in one last sight of her, Henna doing the same. The curve of her cheek and the little dark mole in the hollow beneath her earlobe, the gold and green shards in her eyes, the fringe he wanted to push back from her forehead, the lips he had not nearly kissed enough… His hand fisted at his side and, without another word, he turned on his heel and left.

Henna watched him go, her heart breaking into a thousand pieces as Freya came to stand beside her, looking between her brother's retreating form and Henna, a worried look in her eyes.

'Henna—'

Whatever Freya had been about to say was stopped by the bright smile Henna pasted on her lips. She took her friend's hands in her own, pulling them to her chest, and willed Freya not to ask. Because she would want to seek solace with her friend, to tell her everything, all the things that she could never take back, but she would never betray Aleksander like that. So if Freya asked she would have to lie, and Henna really didn't want to lie.

As if understanding, Freya freed her hand and rubbed a gentle circle against her back, the soothing gesture one she remembered from years before her father passed, and it made her want to cry all over again.

'Are you ready for the engagement party tomorrow night?' Freya asked.

Henna let out a teary laugh. 'It's *your* party, Freya.'

'Yes,' she replied, unable to hide the love and joy that shone from her like a lamp in the darkness. It hurt Henna to want to shy from it, aching that she couldn't feel that same sense of light, but she wouldn't turn from her friend's happiness. She deserved it so, so much.

'Freya, do you think you'd mind if I left a little earlier than planned?'

'From the party?'

Henna shook her head. If nothing else, what she'd just shared with Aleksander was a goodbye and she couldn't bear to work out the next two weeks of her notice.

'You go whenever you need to, Henna, but...' Freya looked at her as if wanting to say something but deciding against it.

'Freya?'

Losing the fight against whatever held her back, Freya said, 'Are you sure you want to do this? *Really* sure? There are so many things you could do.'

Surprised by what Freya had *not* said, it took her a moment to orientate back to her question. 'It's such an amazing opportunity. And I like helping people.' The words had come automatically, from a place of ease rather than of thought. And the look Freya gave her said as much.

'But you don't need to hide behind someone else to help people the way you could. You are a woman of considerable means,' Freya reminded her gently. 'Means that you could make work the way you want them to. Just think about it?'

Freya smiled, pulling her back across the threshold of her office and into the party, while Henna worked to ignore the afterimage her words had left in her mind.

* * *

The following evening Henna unzipped the white covering over the dress she'd chosen for Freya's engagement ball, the strange sense of déjà vu unsettling her. Usually she would have worn a dress that was unobtrusive, that would have disappeared into the background, leaving her faceless and unremarkable to the other guests. But, as of one hour ago, she was no longer employed by the Svardian royal family and was now welcome as a guest to her best friend's engagement party. The knowledge of that had been the impetus behind her unusual purchase.

For many years Henna had ignored the account that she had accessed when she'd withdrawn the money needed to gain entry to the private tables at the casino in Macau. At first, she had seen it as her father's money and she hadn't wanted it or anything to do with it. It had been a poor replacement for the man who had loved her with such strength that she still felt it now. And as the years had gone by it had been pushed to the back of her mind, mainly because she simply hadn't needed it. Freya had offered her the role as lady-in-waiting as soon as she had finished university, her housing was included with the position, her expenditure was minimal.

But Freya was right. Henna *was* a woman of considerable means. And while she hadn't quite worked out what that meant to her yet, she had known that this evening she had wanted, *needed*, to look stunning. It was a vanity, but it was also an armour. Aleksander would be presenting Tuva Paulin at the ball and while Henna knew she would be forgiven for not going, she also knew that she needed to see it. Needed to face this so that she could finally draw a line in the sand between herself and Aleksander, the present and the future. It would hurt, yes, but hopefully it would also cauterise her wounded heart so that she might go on.

She slipped the white garment bag from the hanger to reveal the midnight-blue dress she'd been unable to resist buying. Somewhere in there was the dress she had worn to Macau, the same midnight-blue silk at the very core of the dress, but embellished with a million sequins and sparkles. A thousand layers of embroidered tulle cascaded from the waist into a skirt fit for a princess, falling into a slight train that would fan out on the floor behind her.

Henna reached up to feel the exquisite beading and stitching that reminded her of the sky from the cabin's window in Öström. The texture beneath her palm, sharp and smooth, grounded her. She felt as if this dress told her story, her journey to here, where even though it would hurt and quite possibly damage her heart irrevocably, she would still have the power to stand and bear it. This dress made her feel strong and feminine and courageous—all things that had been in her but hidden…until now.

On the other side of the palace, Aleksander looked out of the window, unseeing of the grounds wrapped in the night's darkness. There was a strange sense of numbness to the evening. Freya's joy had been inescapable since her return from her time away with Kjell, and she had extracted promises from him to visit the cabin in Sweden that she had fallen so in love with. And Aleksandar was glad. Glad that she had Kjell, glad that Marit had Lykos—the latter couple arriving soon.

Aleksander had orchestrated situations that had thrust both of his sisters into the arms of men who loved and valued them beyond compare, which *some* might call manipulation, but that Freya and Marit knew love, thrived in that love, was the one bright light in his life so he was at peace with his actions. Time and time again it had been proved to Aleksander that people could not be trusted to make the right decisions, for themselves or others. He engineered situations where he could be sure of an outcome that would benefit everyone. But as he thought of the last situation he had engineered, he wondered if perhaps he had been wrong to do it. His conscience twisted in warning, but it was too late to change it.

The mantel clock, a present from an old British prime minister, chimed its way through seven tolls and the red-haired woman on the sofa behind him shifted.

'Are you sure this is what you want?' Tuva asked.

It didn't matter what he wanted. It was what was needed.

'Absolutely.'

## CHAPTER ELEVEN

IF THE VÅRBOLL had been exquisite, Freya and Kjell's engagement party was nothing short of magnificent. Having done much of the preparation for it before Freya had left with Kjell, Henna got goosebumps looking at the Rilderdal Palace ballroom. Huge wide strips of white tulle were draped from the ceiling below strings of fairy lights, creating an illuminated vee between each of the chandeliers. Freya had requested boughs of Norwegian spruce and trails of ivy throughout, bringing the outside in and achieving a magical quality to the decorations. Even the staff passing round canapés and drinks had been caught staring at the beauty of it.

Henna smiled. Freya and Kjell deserved nothing less. Breaking a little with tradition, they had been the first in the room, there to welcome every single guest personally. It was what made Freya such a well-loved princess, the personal touch she afforded to everyone equally. Marit and Lykos appeared at the back of the ballroom, clearly not wanting to interrupt the line waiting to wish the happy couple their best. Something in Henna's chest eased at the realisation that this was the first time all the siblings would be together since Aleksander's coronation. Whether his sisters knew or not, he needed it, needed them by his side. Because while he might feel threatened by emotion, he was completely fuelled by it, or it never would have mattered to him who his sisters had married.

Marit approached with Lykos, her eyes staring holes into the back of her sister's head until Freya turned and gave her an affectionate wave before returning to her duty. Only a year ago, Henna knew Marit would have seen it as a dismissal, not being secure enough in herself or the love of her family, but Lykos had come along and stolen her on her wedding day—*twice*—and changed that for her.

Marit pulled Henna into a fierce hug and whispered, 'You can't go. I won't let you.'

Tears threatened to spill at the strong bond of love she felt between them. 'Oh, Marit.'

'What are we going to do without you?' she demanded, pulling back.

'You don't need me any more,' Henna replied, with a smile at the Greek billionaire beside Marit.

'It is nice to finally meet the famous Henna I've heard so much about,' he said, inclining his head over her hand as if to kiss it.

Charmed instantly by the old-fashioned gesture, she replied, 'Likewise.'

As Marit regaled her with stories of Paris and Milan and Athens, Henna realised that the fear she'd had of being only a tool, someone to rely on, to achieve things for Freya and Henna was gone. The easy conversation and the shared humour erased that fear and healed something deep within her, not completely but enough to see things a little more clearly than she had done in the past. She was just about to check on the catering when—

'Who is that?' Marit demanded, looking up to the first-floor balcony.

There was only one possible answer.

'Your brother's guest is Tuva Paulin,' she replied, bracing herself as she turned to face Aleksander and his future fiancée.

Aleksander stood at the top of the stairs, able to see that his sister only had two more couples to greet before he could make his entrance. Tuva's hand was tucked into the crook of his arm, on the side opposite his sword. Everything about this evening had to be perfect. It would set the tone for Freya and Kjell's future—ensuring that, no matter what, she would have the support of the royal family, and hopefully the country, behind her when facing the announcement that she was unable to have children naturally.

Tuva cleared her throat quietly beside him and he realised that the music had transitioned to announce his arrival. He just stopped himself from clenching the fist by his side, gave Tuva a smile and then led them down the grand staircase. Freya and Kjell stood at the bottom on one side and Marit and Lykos on the other and for a second he allowed himself to feel the simple joy of having both of his sisters here with him.

*Family.* He wanted them near, not because it would look good for the country, or bolster his image, as his parents would have suggested. But because he loved them. For the first time he wondered what it would have been like if he'd been able to talk to them about what happened in the past. Whether he would have been this emotionally closed off. Whether he might have healed enough to...

He looked up just at that moment and the sight of Henna stopped his thoughts and his heart. In the second it took to take her in, a kaleidoscope of images from their time away pressed against the back of his eyes. The midnight-blue silk of her dress in Macau, the stars in the sky over Öström, the way her blue skirt parted either side of her legs before he tasted her, how the straps of blue silk had slipped from her shoulders in the elevator, how she had stood there, bearing the weight of his fevered gaze, strong and powerful, daring him to be even remotely worthy of her—the way she was looking at him now.

Gentle pressure pulled at his arm and everything came back in a rush, the musical accompaniment, the sounds of the guests, the trace of concern in Freya's knowing gaze, the painfully perfect smile of the woman beside him. The woman who would be beside him in everything to come. He wasn't fool enough to compare her to Henna. Tuva would lose every time, in every way but one.

Tuva's gaze was heavy on him as he introduced her to his sisters and their partners. Both Kjell and Lykos were still a little wary of him—as they should be—but if Freya and Marit noticed, they didn't let on. Lykos whispered something to Marit and with a long, surprisingly serious glance from his sister, Marit enticed Tuva and Freya away, leaving the three men alone.

A server appeared with a tray of drinks and all three men chose whisky over champagne.

'Something on your mind, Livas?' Aleksander said before a tipped salute of his glass to his future brothers and taking a mouthful of peat, vanilla and burn.

Kjell, ever the military strategist, seemed content to have one eye on them and the other on his fiancée.

'Kozlov.' The word dropped like a bullet from the Greek billionaire's mouth.

Aleksander glared at him but, even without looking at the Viscount of Fjalir beside him, it was eminently clear he had no wish to discuss the matter in public.

The silver-eyed Greek shrugged. 'Kjell is now family. Marit is…teaching me the importance of it and I am embracing it.'

Aleksander looked at Kjell, who held his gaze. 'Russian oligarch, billionaire several times over, questionable dealings in the Ukraine, morally abominable and violent towards women. Nasty piece of work,' Kjell concluded his accurate précis on the man.

Lykos leaned his head towards the man as if to say, *see?*

'He will soon experience the loss of several major contracts that have, until now, afforded him a level of financial security,' said Aleksander, giving in to the bonds that would tie him to even more people.

'And with blood in the water, the sharks will start to circle. Good,' Lykos said with a finality that appeased both men's need for vengeance.

'What you choose to do and who you choose to do it with in your free time is all on you,' Kjell stated, leaning a little close to Aleksander's secrets for his liking. But the man had been a Lieutenant Colonel in the Svardian army, so Aleksander trusted him more than most.

'So, you chose Tuva then?' Lykos observed.

'Not who I was expecting,' Kjell commented. 'You?' he asked the Greek.

It was on the tip of his tongue to demand to know what they were talking about, when he found both of their gazes locked onto where Henna was talking to a clearly besotted French Ambassador.

'No. Shame.'

'Agreed.'

With the distinct impression that they were ganging up on him, Aleksander stalked off, ignoring the sound of gentle laughter behind him, and went to find Tuva.

* * *

Henna extracted herself from the French Ambassador, whose crush on her was nothing but sweet harmlessness. She was just about to find Freya when the music quietened in preparation for the first dance. This was it. This was the line in the sand that Henna needed. This was the inescapable truth that he would never be hers.

The three siblings took up positions around the dance area of the ballroom. It looked like an image from a period drama, the stunning perfection of the clothes—Kjell in military dress uniform, while Lykos Livas shone just as gloriously in his tux. And the women—Henna bit her lip until she tasted a faint metallic thread, releasing it as the sharp sting struck. Tuva was beautiful and poised, perfection in a cream gown that matched Aleksander's ceremonial uniform. They stood in a tableau, waiting for the music to begin, and for a moment she wondered if perhaps this was a dream. That this was where she would wake, but no. The music started and the couples spun around the floor in perfect synchronicity.

And even though she knew that she was strong, knew that she would survive this, she was once again on the outside looking in and it hurt like a thousand cuts to her soul. Aleksander never once made eye contact, but she felt his focus like a touch, slipping down the nape of her neck, her spine, spanning her shoulder blades and holding her in place. Holding her to the press of a body that would never be there.

Would never hold her again. Would never pleasure her or protect her.

Her phone vibrated in her clutch and, as if ready for any possible excuse to break the hold he had on her, she reached in to check her screen. It was a reply to her request to begin her new role as soon as possible. Quickly putting in her code, she read the email, knowing that even if her request had been denied she'd be leaving first thing in the morning. Because, no matter what, she wasn't a masochist. She'd needed to see this, to feel it as real and know it as truth, but…

Her thoughts trailed off as she reread the email. *No.*

She read it again, fury painting her cheeks with a flush.

Your email couldn't have been more fortuitous— if you can start at the beginning of next week it would be greatly welcome. We're so pleased that HRH recommended you and he was right, you really are a godsend!

Her knuckles turned white around the phone. She had, until now, believed that she had been headhunted because of her reputation, because of her skill. She'd thought it had been fortuitous. A sign that she should reach for more while connecting to her mother, even. But all this time it had been Aleksander. He'd kept that from her. Lied to her. Manipulated her into thinking that leaving was her choice, when he'd arranged the entire charade.

She looked up, the full horror of it dawning on her. He'd taken the first opportunity he could to remove her from the Palace. Once his sisters were settled and they no longer needed her, she was nothing to him but a distraction. Expendable and removable. In the way. Just like she had always been.

For the first time that night, his eyes found hers, the bitter chocolate a harsh taste to swallow. Turning from the room, blind to the guests, she picked up her skirts and ran, tears clouding her vision and pain tearing her heart apart.

Aleksander felt a knife pierce his chest when he saw the expression on Henna's face. He knew it wasn't because he was dancing with Tuva, he knew it was something else, something more. She'd been holding her phone and... He didn't even realise he'd left Tuva and was halfway across the ballroom floor, following hot on Henna's heels before it was too late. He heard the gasps and whispers around him as he pursued her out of the door and down a corridor.

His pulse pounded wildly in his veins, fear and hurt coagulating, making his blood thick and hard to push around his body. Everything in him told him it was fruitless. Everything in him told him to let her go, but he couldn't. For all his determination to keep her at arm's length, to push her away even, now, when it came down to it, he couldn't let her go.

Leaving the sounds of the ballroom behind him, he entered the staff wing of the Palace, following the clip of Henna's heels ahead of him. He spun blindly round another corner in the maze of corridors, following the way she led until they were deep in the heart of the Palace. He quickened his pace, no longer able to hold himself back, but she had too. Was she running from him?

The thought spurred him on, until he rounded a corner and came to a sudden stop, seeing her standing there, braced to confront him, fury and accusation shining in her eyes. He wavered, needing to close the distance between them.

'Henna—'

'How could you? How could you do that to me?'

He shook his head. 'Henna, you knew that—'

'I'm not talking about Tuva!' she yelled.

Force of habit had him quickly scanning the corridor for staff or guests, not even half as relieved as he should be to find it empty. They couldn't stay out here. He shoved at a door to the side, opening into an empty office. Satisfied, he grasped her hand and guided her away from ruination for them both. He kicked the door closed behind them and stared at Henna, her chest heaving with her ragged breaths, fury riding hard in her eyes.

'What happened?' he demanded.

'Do you not know already, Your Highness?'

He clenched his jaw, the lashing bitterness in her tone painful because he was sure he had put it there.

'After all, you pride yourself on ensuring that you know every move a person will make before they make it, do you not?'

Realisation crept into his thoughts. She knew. She knew he had engineered the job offer.

As if she saw the train of his thoughts, she nodded. 'How could you do that? Of all the things that you have planned and manipulated, this was particularly cruel.'

He flinched, unable to deny her accusation.

'You move people around a chessboard so that they cannot hurt you, but do you ever think how much hurt you cause?' Henna demanded.

'All the time,' he growled, the confession wrenched from the deepest part of him. 'It is all I *ever* think about.'

She shook her head, clearly disbelieving his words, her eyes full of a pain that swarmed around her like a tornado. 'Was it *all* a lie?'

'I have *never* lied to you.'

'You told me that I would always have a home here!' she cried, her hurt stabbing daggers into his soul. 'That was a lie!'

'Henna—'

'You let me believe that I would be safe here and the entire time, the *entire* time, you were planning for me to take a job in another country!'

'Henna, you earned that role, you *deserve* that role.' He was desperate for her to know that.

'But the price of it is here! The cost of it is to know that you didn't want me here!' she threw at him.

Rage tore through him. Anger, frustration and helplessness. 'You're right, Henna, I didn't want you here. I *don't* want you here.' She reared back as if he had physically struck her. 'How on earth am I supposed to find a fiancée when you are less than five corridors away from me? How am I supposed to be the king that I need to be when you are making me feel everything that I have spent years trying to forget? Tell me, Henna, because if you can make it happen then stay, by all means.'

He had shocked her into silence and he took full advantage. 'Even before Öström, even before we kissed, even before Freya was engaged, I knew that you were more of a threat to me than anyone I had ever known. Even then I knew that you—alone in an entire palace of people—would see the truth. That my need to control everything is beyond trust, beyond betrayal—' His breath shuddered in his lungs. 'Because if I let myself feel for you, then how will I not be destroyed by the feelings I have for…for…my child?' he demanded. 'The decision that was made for me, *without my choice*, was done so that I could rule this country. That can and will only ever be my one purpose now.'

She stared at him, as if sifting through his words, seeing to his soul, and finding him wanting. 'So you refuse to acknowledge your grief and loss and guilt and love and all the things that make us human, because you think it makes you a better king?' she asked incredulously.

'If that is what I need to do, then I shall do it.'

'That is a poor way of honouring the loss of your child.' Her words slapped him so viciously he took a step back, an irrevocable wound cutting into his heart. 'You were a lost teenager then, isolated from the very people who should have helped you and vulnerable to your grief. So you hid it deep down, untouched and unacknowledged. I understand that. You weren't strong enough then, but you are now. And you know better now.'

'Get out,' he whispered, with no less power in his words than the force of a tsunami.

And still she stood against him, immovable, her power that strong.

'I am your *King*!' he yelled.

'And if you say that enough times, will you finally believe that it is an excuse for your manipulations? For taking the same choice away from others that you were denied yourself?' she demanded, seeing straight to the heart of him.

'Don't,' he warned.

'Don't what? Challenge you? Question you? Are you such an autocrat that you would rule by your will alone?'

He took a step back as she took one forward.

'It is time for you to honour your pain and hurt

and guilt. Use the support you have around you now, overcome it and be better for it. You deserve it, and so do they.'

He shook his head as if trying to ward off her words.

'Can't you see? If you did, then you would know that you are loved, that…that *I* love you,' she said, her words penetrating the walls he was hastily building around his heart.

Aleksander shook his head and Henna tried to hold her heart together even as it slipped through her fingers like sand. The pain was incalculable, tearing and ripping at her even as she stood before him.

'You don't,' he replied.

She let out a helpless laugh. 'It's not something you have the power to control this time, Aleksander.'

A look of determined sincerity passed over his features. 'I know,' he said, as if finally admitting a limit to his authority. 'But I was telling the truth. You don't love me. You love the boy who found you in the maze, who introduced you to his sister. That boy, he was funny and charming and easygoing, but I am not that boy any more. What happened to me changed me on a fundamental level.'

If he had been angry, if he had hurled accusations or manipulated her words, she would have something to fight against. But this? This was a surrender she didn't know what to do with, and no matter how much she tried she couldn't stop the pain pouring from her heart like life blood.

'You have built a dream around me and it's time for you to wake up,' he said, his words and tone gentle but so unbelievably destructive.

Tears filled her vision and he reached out for her, but she pulled away before he could make contact. She wanted to deny it, she wanted to refuse what he was saying was true, but could she? Yes, she had looked and looked for the boy who had given her so much, but had she been so desperate that she had made it all up? Imagined the man she had fallen in love with? Had she done it again and built herself a future around a man she thought would never hurt her?

Her chest ached and her head hurt and she looked deep into her heart and knew the truth. 'I told you that I loved you because you deserved to know. But I deserve *more*,' she said, and turned from the room and the man she loved, but not before she saw the look of devastation in his eyes.

Henna slipped through the quiet Palace, most of her belongings already packed and sent ahead to her hotel. She retrieved her bag and coat from her now empty suite and a taxi was waiting for her at the staff entrance. She didn't turn, didn't pause, didn't slow as she made her way towards the car waiting on the gravel driveway. And as the clock chimed midnight from within the Palace, Henna didn't even look back. The past was gone and only the future lay before her, even if it broke her heart.

# CHAPTER TWELVE

ALEKSANDER STARED AT the door Henna had left through for what felt like hours, his mind spending every second of that time replaying what she had said, what he had said…why it had happened and how. Two steps ahead—he had always been two steps ahead, but this time he was very much behind.

Even though he knew that there could never have been another outcome, his mind processed an infinite number of scenarios that might have ended differently. If he hadn't said… If she'd just… Each one made his head and heart hurt more and more.

On numb legs he forced himself from the room and found his way back to his quarters. He slammed the door shut behind him and was halfway across the living room when he realised that Freya was standing beside the fireplace and Marit sat at the end of the sofa, both staring at him with accusation in their eyes.

He sighed and bit out a curse. 'What do you want?' he demanded.

'We want—'

'To know if you are okay,' Marit said, her worried words cutting off Freya's angry outburst. He was sure that Freya had plenty to say, and not just because he'd ruined her engagement party.

'Oh, God,' he said, hands bracketing his temples, just realising what a monumental mess he'd made of things. 'How bad is it?' he asked, perching on the arm of a sixteenth century chaise longue.

'Tuva told everyone it was food poisoning, so there's that,' Freya revealed.

'Food poisoning?' He barked out a laugh—the last thing he thought he'd be doing that evening.

'There may have been a little glee on her part in sharing such a…frank explanation for your disappearance,' Freya replied, her own delight very close to the surface. 'And I suppose it's less embarrassing than being run out on by the King of Svardia.'

Guilt dug into his stomach and he groaned, bracketing his temples with his fingers. He felt his sister's hand on his shoulder.

'Tuva will be fine,' Freya said, trying to reassure him. 'When we left, she seemed to be having *quite* the conversation with the Austrian Ambassador.'

Nevertheless, Aleksander promised himself he'd find a way to make it up to her.

'Yes, but never mind all that,' Marit said. 'Are you okay?'

It was on the tip of his tongue to dismiss his

sisters' concern, but Henna's words came back to haunt him.

*'You know better now.'*

*'Use the support you have around you now...'*

Henna was right, he realised with a shocking twist of the knife deep in his heart.

He shook his head slowly. 'No, I don't think I am,' he replied to Marit's question. And finally, after twelve years, he slowly told them the story of what had happened to him, to Kristine, about the pregnancy and how it had affected the years that followed. How he had shut everyone out because it was easier to close off all emotion than to open up to even the smallest amount of hurt. How he'd felt it was the only way for him to rule. How it had led to this—his search for someone to marry who didn't engage him emotionally—and how he'd arranged for Henna to be offered a position elsewhere.

'She is my friend, Sander.' Her words were an accusation but her use of his childhood nickname warmed a part of him he'd thought frozen solid a long time ago. 'You should not have done that.'

Everything in him wanted to refute her accusation. He rubbed his chest. He'd been so focused on not letting anyone close enough to inflict the kind of hurt that he had experienced, the hurt he had inflicted on Kristine, that he hadn't realised how Henna had already slipped into his palace and his heart and become irrevocably lodged there. It was she who had made him feel safe, she who had enticed his trust, she who had been more than his equal, who inspired him to be and do better. And he had betrayed her in the most painful and deepest way.

He cursed.

'I think he's getting it.'

'Shame it's a little late,' groused Freya.

'Oh, give him a moment,' Marit scolded. 'He's learning.'

Ignoring their chatter, Aleksander thought through his options. Henna had been right, of course, about everything—but, most importantly, about finally facing his feelings about the past.

'I need…' He looked up to find his sisters waiting expectantly.

'Whatever it is, we're here and we'll help,' Freya said, reaching for him and pulling him into a hug.

'Oh, you guys!' Marit cried, before trying to stretch her arms around them both, and they descended into teary-eyed giggles. Well, the girls did. Aleksander would never admit to such a thing.

Two days later, Aleksander watched from the back of his car as the man said goodbye to his children, got in his car and left for work. He waited another five minutes to make sure the man didn't return and if Aleksander needed that time to steel himself, then that was what he needed. He was done denying the things he felt and although he knew that this might be one of the hardest things he'd ever do, he knew it was one of the most important. Not just in his hope to get Henna back, but for himself too.

He exited the car and approached the modest two-storey home. His close protection officers were present but discreet, knowing how important it was that this remained away from the public eye. Not for him but for the woman in the house and her family. His footsteps sounded loud on the paving stones that led up to the front door in the quiet of the early morning and, before he could think again, he knocked on the door.

Kristine opened it and for a moment there was shock in her gaze and then an understanding so acute and so empathetic he nearly buckled under the weight of it and when she smiled he felt tears stinging the backs of his eyes.

'Can you come in?' she asked, her gaze looking for the protection officers she knew would be there.

'If that is okay?'

'Aleks, come in,' she said, as if telling him off and welcoming him at the same time. She stood back from the door and he entered her home. She ushered him into a sitting room filled with toys and sofas and pictures and DVDs and books and all the things that seemed so normal he ached.

A little blond boy came running into the room, took one wide-eyed look at him and made to run back out again, before being scooped up by his mother.

'Dani, this is an old friend of Mummy's. Say hello,' she said.

'Hello,' came the shy response, and it took a second try for Aleksander to greet Kristine's son, but he did.

She sent him off to play with his older siblings, before seeming awkward for the first time. 'Can I get you tea, or coffee?'

'No, thank you,' he said, shaking his head. 'How are you?'

She smiled and gestured for him to take a seat on the sofa, which he did when she took the armchair. 'Good,' she said, nodding. 'I'm good. How are *you*?'

'Is it that obvious?' he asked ruefully.

'Only because you're here.'

He nodded. 'I have some things I want to say, if that's okay?'

'Of course it is, Aleks.'

He twisted his hands, forgetting to stop himself before the sign of his feelings could show. His throat was thick and rough, but his words came out clear. 'I'm so sorry. I'm sorry you had to make that decision. I'm sorry that I didn't, couldn't, protect you from that.'

'Aleks. I don't blame you. I never did. I thought...' She trailed off, but he understood.

'You thought I blamed you?' he asked. She nodded. 'I couldn't,' he replied quickly. 'Ever. I understand why you made the decision you did. I just... You should never have been in a position to make that decision—alone. Or, worse, with pressure from my father.' He could barely bring himself to say the words.

'Your father made it clear that he would honour any choice I made, and that I would have his support. He is not a bad man, but I know that it must have been difficult growing up with him.'

Relief hit him, so strong that if Aleksander hadn't been sitting he might have fallen. But his smile was sad. 'It wasn't easy, but this helps a little.' She understood, he could see that. 'I loved you,' he said, feeling it even now, but as a faint echo, something similar but in no way close to the other love burning bright in his heart.

'I know. I felt it. I loved you too. But we were too young. And…' She paused, as if unsure whether to say her next words or not. 'And I would never have been your Queen,' she said sadly.

He shook his head. He understood that too. In some ways, not having a normal ending to their relationship had meant it was stuck in time, leaving him unable to heal and grieve and recover like he might have done otherwise.

'Who is she?'

His head jerked up to see her gentle affection for him.

'I imagine,' Kristine continued, 'that, whoever it is, she is the one who helped you find your way here.'

This time he smiled. 'Henna Olin.'

'I remember her,' Kristine replied fondly.

'You do?' he asked, surprised.

'Yes, of course. She could never take her eyes off you.'

They caught up for a short while after, talking on the past, on their families, both knowing that this would likely be the last time they would see each other. Aleksander made sure that he left nothing unsaid, and when he returned to the car that would take him back to the Palace he felt as if he was finally ready to face the hardest fight he would ever have.

Because he had no intention of letting Henna go.

She could have used her keys but had chosen to ring the bell, so waited for one of the staff her stepmother employed to answer the door. The maid looked at Henna curiously and asked if she could be of help, clearly not recognising her.

Henna couldn't work out if it was funny or desperately sad that the people who occupied her childhood home didn't know her. Viveca appeared behind the woman and said, 'Oh, it's you. Come in then,' and disappeared off towards the living area, or at least where it had once been.

As Henna crossed the threshold she was torn between how big her father's estate was, but how small everything looked. It felt as if she was viewing it through a different lens than the last time she'd been here, her focus narrowed by loss. Twin strands of grief wrapped themselves around her, giving her just enough space to move, but nothing near the freedom she needed.

'What are you doing here? Mother's out, if that's who you were after,' called the disembodied voice, the monied, aristocratic accent sharp enough to cut glass. It had struck Henna a little while after she had joined the Palace staff that, for all the superiority and class Viveca and her mother wore like mink, they had nothing of the class she had witnessed through the years. A class not born from wealth or status, but rooted in kindness, grace and generosity.

She was glad in that moment that her father had never discovered the truth about the person he had entrusted with the care of his child—he would have been devastated. She looked around the large entrance hall that he had chased her through playing tag, the memory of their joint laughter fading in her ears but strong in her heart. And now she realised that she had not come here to get the last of her things, she had come here to say goodbye.

As if drawn by her silence, Viveca appeared, drenched in pale silk and fur, wearing crimson lipstick and cruelty in her eyes. 'Well, has the stupidity in your brain finally taken over your tongue? What are you doing here?' she demanded, as if Henna didn't have a right to be in her family home—her *father's* home.

'What was it?' Henna asked, stopping Viveca mid-turn, having become bored waiting for an answer. When Henna finally had her attention she pressed on. 'What was it that I did to you that filled you with such hatred?'

'You mistake yourself. You are so insignificant to me that I can't even summon up enough energy to hate you.'

'So you are simply this mean to everyone?' Henna asked.

'How dare you?' Viveca screeched, charging towards Henna across the black and white checked flooring of the hallway. 'Is this because of Nils? Have you finally decided to grow a backbone?'

There was a temptation to be cruel. To meet her poisoned barbs with taunts just as cutting and hurtful—to belittle Viveca. But that wasn't who Henna was and it certainly wasn't who she wanted to be. She'd told Aleksander that she knew how to deal with bullies, but she had been lying. She had never dealt with Viveca. Ignoring her hadn't made her go away. It hadn't made her any less hurtful or mean.

'No, this is not because of Nils,' she replied truthfully as the scales fell from her eyes. She *had* been lying to herself, just as Aleksander had accused, only not about her feelings for him. Being here after her father's death, with Viveca and her stepmother, had been awful. Truly awful. But making herself useful to them, making herself invisible to them, had pacified the two to the point where it had made Henna's life easier. And somewhere along the line it had become habit. It had become her way of being.

She had told herself that she liked helping people and being efficient because that was how she'd survived Viveca and her mother, but was it true?

Was it what she wanted? Or had she simply been on autopilot?

She was distracted from unravelling her thoughts by her stepsister, who pulled up just short of invading her personal space.

'Or maybe it is,' Henna said, Viveca's betrayal with Nils leading her back to her childhood. 'Because I want to know what it was that I had that you wanted so much that you needed to steal something else from me.'

Viveca looked as if she had been struck, the sting bringing a sheen of unshed tears to her vivid blue gaze. '*Everything*,' she answered after a heartbeat. 'Everything. He may have died when you were young, but your father—he loved you. You couldn't stop *telling us* just how much he loved you. Your perfect father. Mine?' She laughed, bitterness and pain audible in her tone. 'He left. Walked out when I was four and that was the last time I saw him.' Henna took a step forward, but Viveca held up a hand to ward her off. 'And *then*,' she said, the meanness returning to her voice, 'you took Aleksander. He was supposed to be mine. Mother said. She'd wanted *me* to befriend him at that party, not you!'

All the violence and rage she saw in Viveca in that moment teetered on the brink of turning on Henna or turning back on herself and for a moment Henna felt a crawling fear scratching at the back of her neck, before she shoved it aside. There was nothing to fear here now, and truly she only felt sorry for Viveca.

All that anger and hurt… And her mother had been no kind, loving or generous presence in Viveca's life at all.

No, she wouldn't forgive her for sleeping with Nils, but that kind of hurt had rotted something deep within Viveca. Aleksander might have buried his, locked his away, but he'd never been mean with it. He had hurt her, yes, but it hadn't been an act of cruelty. She could see now that it had been an act of self-preservation. And in his own way he had tried—as he had with his sisters—to give her something else. To nudge her towards a position and role that she had genuinely been interested in.

'Viveca, if you ever want to change the way things are between us I would be open to that,' she said, thinking of how she felt about Freya and Marit and hoping that if Viveca did ever confront her demons they might at least become friends.

Viveca frowned, as if not understanding or believing her words and, before she could be stopped, Henna swept her up in a fierce hug, before leaving and not looking back. There was nothing more here for Henna. It hadn't been her home for a very long time. Now, she wanted to look to her future.

*'Are you sure you want to do this?'*

Freya's question sounded in her ears. She was still excited by the prospect of the role waiting for her in London. But Henna needed a little more time. Seeing Viveca, coming here…it had cleared the path to making a decision. Yes, Aleksander's betrayal had cut deep, even now she felt the sting and burn in her chest, as if she'd inhaled winter's bite. Her heart had broken, but her soul had kept her standing and she owed it to herself to fight for the very best for herself. In her heart, her father smiled and some of the pain from the loss of Aleksander eased just a little.

Can you meet me in the maze? I need to talk to you privately but I can't leave the Palace. Please, Henna, I wouldn't ask if it wasn't desperately important. F xx

It was the day before her flight and the last thing Henna wanted was to return to Rilderdal Palace, but Freya had sworn that Aleksander was away on business. She hadn't even wanted that much information because her mind had quickly filled with questions about the organisation, whether Kozlov had kept his word, whether Tuva was with him…

Henna had refused to read any newspapers, listen to any news reports. Her only social media had been through the palace communications team so even that was closed to her now. She felt oddly isolated and out of tune with Svardia and hoped it was for the best, even if it felt wrong deep in her heart. The car Freya had sent for her passed smoothly through Security and took the private road access to leave her just beside the maze.

Unable to resist, her hand reached out to swipe across the hundreds and thousands of tiny little vivid green leaves. They tickled her palm like the memories playing in her mind. As a child, the walls of the maze had towered over her. They were still taller than her, but only just, which made them feel so much less intimidating.

She peered into the entrance and called out for Freya, but heard no response. Was she supposed to meet her here or at the centre? Henna checked her watch and, hating the idea of keeping Freya waiting, she started on the path she had forced herself to learn after getting lost. She had discovered that it had been designed as a labyrinth rather than a maze, there being only one true path to the centre, with many dead ends and confusing junctions along the way.

As she followed the route she knew in her mind, she couldn't help but feel that she was taking the first steps on the right path of her own journey and she was excited to tell Freya what she'd decided about her future. Henna was lost in the thought of her best friend's reaction when she turned into the heart of the maze, so it took her a moment to register what she was seeing.

Aleksander had clearly been pacing back and forth, but he stopped the moment she emerged at the centre of the maze. She had never seen him like this. His hair was messy and his shirtsleeves rolled back. His fists clenched and unclenched at his sides, and even then he *still* looked devastatingly hand-some. The sun glinted on the golden strands of his hair, and the flex of tension in his jaw only served to make him look glorious. Henna shook her head,

intensely disliking the fact that she hadn't built up
an immunity to him.

'What am I doing here, Aleksander?' she demanded, hurt and angry that he would do this to
her, manipulate her, *again*.

In that moment Aleksander saw the pain he had
caused Henna. He was struck silent by it and all the
things he had prepared to say, had written and tried
to memorise disappeared. Refusing to wait any longer for his answer, she turned to leave, forcing him
to cross the distance between them in quick strides,
rounding her and cutting off her exit. She had to pull
up short to stop from crashing into him.

His heart pounded at the sight of the dark circles
beneath her eyes, knowing that he deserved to witness her hurt and far, far more. He had manipulated
her and in doing so betrayed her. He had taken her
choice away, just like his had been taken away, and
worse—he had taken away her home. It had scarred
him to his soul that he had done that to her.

'I'm sorry,' he said, the words pouring from his
soul with the most sincerity he'd ever felt. 'I am so
truly sorry.'

'Do you know what you're sorry for?' she asked,
glaring up at him. 'Or are you just saying what you
think I need to hear?'

'I *know*,' he said, reaching for her hand, but she
pulled it away. 'I…there is so much I want to say,
things I'd like to…' He winced. This was coming out

all wrong. As if surprised by his ineloquence, she took a step back from him. 'I went to see Kristine.' The words burst from him, stopping her in her tracks. He could see the questions in her eyes—the concern for him so pure and powerful and clear in her gaze it gave him hope. It made him *stronger*, which he should have realised a long time ago.

'How is she?' Henna asked hesitantly.

'Happy,' he said, finally at peace with the past. 'She loves her quiet life, her husband is kind, her children healthy and delightful. Speaking to her was something I should have done a long time ago. Freya and Marit said the same.'

'You told your sisters about what happened?' Shock filled Henna's question.

'Yes. You were, *unsurprisingly*, right,' he acknowledged. 'I hadn't realised how much I had cut myself off from them until you opened my eyes to it.' He dared to take a step towards her and this time she didn't move away. This time, he opened his heart and bared it to her with his words. 'Henna, for years I thought my grief, my guilt, was a cage. But in truth it was a maze. I just couldn't find the way out, until you.' Henna's eyes grew round with surprise and he pressed on. 'You guided me, like Ariadne—leaving me a string, a thread, for me to follow that led me not just out of the maze, but to you. My strength. My *heart*.'

Her eyes flitted across his face, as if searching for

the truth, and he felt every movement like a touch, like a caress.

'But…but what about Tuva?'

Aleksander shook his head. 'There is no Tuva. There is no one else. And Henna—' he reached for her chin, gently holding her gaze to his, for this was the important bit '—there never will be. If you choose to leave I will understand, but know that there will *never* be anyone else. No other woman will wear my ring, or my crown.'

'But—'

'I love you. You are the *only* person I want by my side,' he said, taking the sudden flare in her eyes as a sign for him to continue. 'For so long I was fighting my feelings for you, I was so busy counting the ways that wanting you, needing you, could hurt me, that I didn't realise the many, *many* ways that you made me better. I was so sure that my love for you made me vulnerable and weak, opening me to manipulation and giving me over to you for you to destroy, I didn't stop to think, to realise, that you would *never* do that to me. The entire time, you gave me the truth when I needed it, and you asked me to share my hurt when I would have buried it. You gave me so much and I…' he struggled, forcing himself to confront his greatest sin, guilt burning and branding him '…I betrayed you. I took away your home, your *safety*, and I will never forgive myself, nor will I dare ask for your forgiveness. But I owe you the greatest apology and I vow to you that, no matter what, you will always

have a home here, in Svardia, in Rilderdal Palace,
you will *always* be part of our family,' he promised,
hoping that she could read the truth in his words.

Shivers broke out over Henna's skin, Aleksander's
words touching her far more deeply than she could
ever have imagined. Her heart was soaring, but her
mind still urged caution. What Aleksander was offering was more than she had ever imagined but…
    'You hurt me.'
    'I know. And I am so, so truly sorry for it. You de-
serve the world, and if you are not by my side please
know that I, Freya and Marit will all help you in
whatever way you want or need. And if you still want
to leave for London then I completely understand.'
    'London?' Henna asked, momentarily confused.
'I'm not going to London,' she said.
    'You're not taking the job?'
    She shook her head. 'I turned it down.'
    'Because of me? Henna—'
    'No—' she couldn't help but laugh '—not because
of you,' she said, her heart easing into the realisation that he loved her. It was an excited, fizzing,
*filling* kind of feeling that she wasn't quite used to
yet. Aleksander searched her gaze and she realised
he was waiting for an explanation. And suddenly
she knew that it was Aleksander she had been waiting to tell. Yes, she would love to tell Freya, but this
moment was what she had wanted since making her
decision about her future. Pride unfurled in her soul,

knowing that she was about to share her plan with someone she respected, someone she wanted to impress but didn't need to. She was excited about the future now and where it would take her. It felt *right*. Just like being in Aleksander's arms.

'I realised that I could do more—*be* more. And... you helped me see that,' she said truthfully. She would have enjoyed the job in London and she most definitely would have excelled in it. But after visiting Viveca, realising that so much of what she thought she wanted had been shaped by habit and denial, she had forced herself to think about what she really wanted to do with her life. 'As you discovered in Macau, I am sitting on a considerably large amount of money. Money I had ignored because it felt wrong, a tainted compensation for the loss of my father.' He reached for her then and pulled her into a hug. She let him hold her as the wash of memories flowed over her, more easily with him by her side.

'But I know now that I can use that money to do some good. That I *want* to do it and be recognised for that myself, not hide in the shadows behind someone else. So I am flying to Paris with meet with Célia d'Argent.'

'Chariton Enterprises?' Aleksander asked, surprised, aware of the excellent reputation of the company that matched wealthy clients with deserving causes.

'Yes. They have a selection of charities for me to consider so that I can help people directly.'

'Any one of them would be lucky to have you,'

he said, his fingers smoothing her hair, a silence descending between them. She felt his breath lock in his lungs, an unspoken question pressing against his lips. Hope and desperation warred in his gaze and she knew what he wanted to ask, was asking—she felt his need as if he were part of her.

She cupped his jaw, connecting her heart to his, her soul to his. 'I love you. You found me when I was lost and you gave me so much. And it helped, it slowly eased my grief, and it was magical and wonderful—the handsome prince who gave me what I needed before I even knew it myself.' His heart pounded beneath the palm of her hand, fierce and strong and all hers.

'Henna Olin,' he asked, eyes bright and full of hope, 'will you do me the greatest honour and allow me to be your husband, your partner, your lover and your home?'

Tears filled her eyes and spilled, and she felt no shame in them because they were true and honest and full of love.

'Yes, Your Majesty. I will.'

And there, in the centre of the maze in the grounds of Svardia's Rilderdal Palace, where they had lost their hearts, only to find them again, Aleksander and Henna didn't have the slightest idea that their love and marriage would soon become a real-life fairytale that generations would grow up knowing and admiring around the world.

# EPILOGUE

HENNA STOOD IN the bedroom doorway in the private wing of Svardia's Rilderdal Palace, watching her husband, the King of Svardia, soothe their son. She leaned her head against the doorframe, the smile familiar on her lips, knowing that she would never forget the sight of him holding their children, never forget the way it made her feel. Henna kept expecting her heart to burst, unable to take any more happiness and love. But, as it had done when Aleksander had proposed, then when they had married, when they'd had their first child, Henriette, and three months ago their son, Jonas, it simply stretched to accommodate as much love as she was capable of feeling.

The last five years had been a whirlwind and there had been times that had sorely tested them both. The news of Freya's fertility difficulties had been accepted mostly with positivity, understanding and compassion. And, despite some tensions and grumbling, Aleksander had passed the legislation changes he'd wanted, removing the title requirements for royal family consorts, but also incorporating the line of succession to include adopted children.

She had taken to the role of Queen Consort surprisingly well, even though Aleksander still joked to anyone who would listen that she was the real power behind the throne. She had decided with Aleksander not to have a coronation ceremony because the planning for the second of their two weddings—the public one—had utterly exhausted her. Especially as she had been in her first trimester at the time. Heads of state had flown in from around the world and Henna had even caught the familiar names of two members she knew belonged to the organisation. It had been watched by more than thirty-two million people worldwide but it still didn't mean as much to her as the small private wedding conducted in the chapel in the Palace grounds two weeks before, with just Aleksander's sisters and their partners in attendance.

Henna had hoped that she might one day be able to create some kind of relationship with her stepsister, but Viveca had remained almost intentionally mean and, while it hurt a little, Henna knew that Viveca's pain was greater. Aleksander had talked it through with her and she knew he thought she was crazy for hoping, but Henna refused to close that door.

For their honeymoon, Aleksander had taken her to London. They had stayed in an apartment in Knightsbridge, done all the touristy things, and then Aleksander had tracked down some information about her mother and where she and her family had lived. They'd visited the area but, understanding her family were no longer there, she hadn't wanted to impose on the new tenants. Henna had thought she might feel a connection to it, but realised that her home wasn't in the memories of the past but in the connections in her present. It was Aleksander, Freya and Marit…it was Svardia, the country and the people.

Aleksander had maintained his twice-yearly visits to Öström and she had gone with him every time, thoroughly enjoying the peace and quiet and relishing the powerful force of nature that was the sea and the tide along that craggy peninsula. Thankfully, no one had heard anything from Ilian Kozlov in the years since his abrupt departure, and every now and then Aleksander persuaded her to play him at cards. Sometimes she won, sometimes he did, but every time it ended up in bed, the cards forgotten and pleasure the last thing on their lips.

She heard the pitter-patter of little feet in the hallway and looked down at the irrepressible mop of blonde curls Henriette had inherited from some long-forgotten family gene.

'Mama,' her daughter whispered, reaching for her hand, 'is Jonas okay?'

Henna swept her daughter up into her arms. 'Of course, Ette. I think he just missed his papa,' she explained with a smile.

'But he's right there,' Ette pointed out as Aleksander turned to face them, Jonas tucked against his chest.

'Which is why he's stopped crying,' Henna whispered to Ette. 'Papa did the same thing for you when you were that small.'

'He did?' Ette asked, beautiful brown eyes big and round.

Aleksander looked up at them and in that moment she knew that her husband felt what she did. Awe that this was theirs—their family, their life. They never took it for granted, all that they had and all the good that they could do. Aleksander had promised to give her a home, one where she would always feel safe and loved in, and he had done just that.

'Are we still going to Narna tomorrow?'

Henna bit her lip, knowing that Ette meant Dalarna, in Sweden, where Kjell and Freya had their cabin. 'Yes, we are,' she said, struggling to keep hold of her when Ette started wriggling in joy.

'We're going to see Alarik and Mikael and Malin?'

Henna nodded. 'And guess what…' she asked her daughter. 'Marit is pregnant!'

'Again?' Ette demanded with excitement.

Henna heard Aleksander stifle a laugh.

'Yes, now, let's say goodnight to Jonas and leave so he can get some sleep.'

Following a very gentle kiss from Ette, Henna took in the sleepy-eyed smiling face of her son, his surprising head of hair all his father's, but his eyes were hazel just like hers. Although she wasn't quite sure how to feel about it, their son had a Pinterest page with more followers than the one of Aleksander's jawline.

She looked up then, caught the love blazing in his eyes for her, for their children, and knew that he was thankful. Thankful for the journey they'd been on together to be here, now, and happy.

'I love you,' he mouthed, not wanting to disturb Jonas.

'I love you too,' she returned. Since his proposal in the maze not a single day had gone by without him telling her that she was loved, and not a single day ever would.

\* \* \* \* \*

*Did you get lost in the magic of*
Claimed to Save His Crown?
*Then make sure to catch*
*the first and second instalments in*
The Royals of Svardia *trilogy*

Snowbound with His Forbidden Princess
Stolen from Her Royal Wedding

*And don't miss these other Pippa Roscoe stories!*

Playing the Billionaire's Game
Terms of Their Costa Rican Temptation
From One Night to Desert Queen
The Greek Secret She Carries
Snowbound with His Forbidden Princess

*Available now!*

**WE HOPE YOU ENJOYED
THIS BOOK FROM**

**◊ HARLEQUIN**

# PRESENTS

*Escape to exotic locations where passion knows no bounds.*

Welcome to the glamorous lives of royals and billionaires,
where passion knows no bounds. Be swept into a world
of luxury, wealth and exotic locations.

**8 NEW BOOKS AVAILABLE EVERY MONTH!**

HPHALO2021

COMING NEXT MONTH FROM

**⊕ HARLEQUIN**

# PRESENTS

### #4041 THE KING'S CHRISTMAS HEIR
*The Stefanos Legacy*
by Lynne Graham
When Lara rescued Gaetano from a blizzard, she never imagined she'd say "I do" to the man with no memory. Or, when the revelation that he's actually a future king rips their passionate marriage apart, that she'd be expecting a precious secret!

### #4042 CINDERELLA'S SECRET BABY
*Four Weddings and a Baby*
by Dani Collins
Innocent Amelia's encounter with Hunter was unforgettable... and had life-changing consequences! After learning Hunter was engaged, she vowed to raise their daughter alone. But now, Amelia's secret is suddenly, scandalously exposed!

### #4043 CLAIMED BY HER GREEK BOSS
by Kim Lawrence
Playboy CEO Ezio will do anything to save the deal of a lifetime. Even persuade his prim personal assistant, Matilda, to take a six-month assignment in Greece...as his convenient bride!

### #4044 PREGNANT INNOCENT BEHIND THE VEIL
*Scandalous Royal Weddings*
by Michelle Smart
Her whole life, Princess Alessia has put the royal family first, until the night she let her desire for Gabriel reign supreme. Now she's pregnant! And to avoid a scandal, that duty demands a hasty royal wedding...

HPCNMRA0822

## #4045 THEIR DESERT NIGHT OF SCANDAL
*Brothers of the Desert*
### by Maya Blake
Twenty-four hours in the desert with Sheikh Tahir is more than Lauren bargained for when she came to ask for his help. Yet their inescapable intimacy empowers Lauren to lay bare the scandalous truth of their shared past—and her still-burning desire for Tahir...

## #4046 AWAKENED BY THE WILD BILLIONAIRE
### by Bella Mason
Colliding with a masked stranger at a ball sends shy Emma's pulse skyrocketing. And that's *before* he introduces himself as Alexander Hastings, the CEO with a wild side, which puts him way out of her league! Will Emma step out of the shadows and into the billionaire's penthouse?

## #4047 THE MARRIAGE THAT MADE HER QUEEN
*Behind the Palace Doors...*
### by Kali Anthony
To claim her crown, queen-to-be Lise must wed. The man she must turn to is Rafe, the self-made billionaire who once made her believe in love. He'll have to make her believe in it again for passion to be part of their future...

## #4048 STRANDED WITH HIS RUNAWAY BRIDE
### by Julieanne Howells
Surrendering her power to a man is unacceptable to Princess Violetta. Even *if* that man sets her alight with a single glance! But when Prince Leo tracks his runaway bride down and they are stranded together, he's not the enemy she first thought...

---

**YOU CAN FIND MORE INFORMATION ON UPCOMING HARLEQUIN TITLES, FREE EXCERPTS AND MORE AT HARLEQUIN.COM.**

HPCNMRB0822

SPECIAL EXCERPT FROM

# ⊕ HARLEQUIN
# PRESENTS

*Colliding with a masked stranger at a ball sends
shy Emma's pulse skyrocketing. And that's before he
introduces himself as Alexander Hastings,
the CEO with a wild side, which puts him
way out of her league! Will Emma step out of the
shadows and into the billionaire's penthouse?*

*Read on for a sneak preview of Bella Mason's
debut story for Harlequin Presents,*
Awakened by the Wild Billionaire.

"Emma," Alex said, pinning her against the wall in a spectacularly graffitied alley, the walls an ever-changing work of art, when he could bear it no more. "I have to tell you. I really don't care about seeing the city. I just want to get you back in my bed."

He could barely believe that he wanted to take her back home. Sending her on her way was the smarter plan. But how smart was it really to deny himself? Emma knew the score. This wasn't about feelings or a relationship. It was just sex.

"Give me the weekend. I promise you won't regret it." His voice was low and rough. He could see in her eyes that she knew just how aroused he was, and with his body against hers, she could feel it.

"I want that too," she breathed.

"What I said before still stands. This doesn't change things."

"I know that." She grinned. "I don't want it to."

*Don't miss*
Awakened by the Wild Billionaire
*available October 2022 wherever*
*Harlequin Presents books and ebooks are sold.*

Harlequin.com

Copyright © 2022 by Bella Mason

HPEXP0822